The Median Line

By the same author:

Slow Burner
The Telemann Touch
Venetian Blind
Closed Circuit
The Arena
The Unquiet Sleep
The High Wire
The Antagonists
The Powder Barrel
The Hard Sell
The Power House
The Conspirators
A Cool Day for Killing
The Doubtful Disciple
The Hardliners
The Bitter Harvest
The Protectors
The Old Masters
The Kinsmen
The Scorpion's Tail
Yesterday's Enemy
The Poison People
Visa to Limbo

The Median Line

William Haggard

CASSELL
LONDON

CASSELL LTD.
35 Red Lion Square, London WC1R 4SG
and at Sydney, Auckland, Toronto, Johannesburg,
an affiliate of
Macmillan Publishing Co., Inc.,
New York.

First published 1979

ISBN 0 304 30464 6

Typeset by Inforum Ltd., Portsmouth
Printed in Great Britain by
The Camelot Press Ltd, Southampton

1

Diplomatic dinner parties were not Colonel Russell's idea of amusement, but this one would be a clear exception, held in an ambassador's house but with none of the spurious pomp he detested, the bitchiness only equalled in showbiz. In fact it was hardly a party at all, just five pleasant people sitting down to a meal.

He read the handwritten letter again. Just the ambassador and of course his wife, and two guests from the ambassador's country. His Excellency was a man Russell liked, for he had none of the airs and affected graces of the profession which he happened to work in, no cultivated ambience of a man apart and therefore significant. His wife was a charming woman, French, and Russell had known her well for some time. He permitted a secret smile. Yes, charming. Did the ambassador know? He rather thought not, for both of them had been very discreet. In any case he would give no sign since he was a civilized and tolerant man, virtues not owned by every Excellency.

He sat down to write a polite acceptance, noting with a quiet approval that a postscript simply said 'Black Tie'. That set the tone of the evening perfectly. Tails suited Russell's still spare figure but he hated the chore of climbing into them, and if any formal invitation should be noted with the word 'Decorations' he would turn it down as a matter of principle. Wearing miniatures with plain clothes was immodest.

Quarter past seven for eight, he noticed. That gave adequate time for a comfortable drink instead of guzzling against the clock. Charles Russell nodded; he would go with great pleasure.

He arrived at seven-fifteen precisely and kissed his hostess's hand unselfconsciously. Her husband brought him a ration of sherry in a flat-bottomed glass holding maybe four ounces. Charles Russell admired the Spanish *copita* but it made for somewhat fussy drinking. This would last him till dinner more than comfortably. There wasn't any servant visible. His Excellency was serving himself.

'I believe you know my wife,' he said. He said it without the hint of an overtone, an oboist blowing an A to tune on.

'We've met once or twice.'

'I'm delighted to hear it. Sometimes I fear I'm obliged to neglect her.' This time the point of the foil was bare and Russell prepared to turn it smoothly. But the thrust never came: H.E. changed the subject. 'Just the five of us tonight,' he said. 'We three and another man you have met. The fifth will be the great man's bodyguard, but pay him no attention whatever. In any case he speaks no language apart from a really shocking Arabic.'

'Interesting,' Russell said.

'You will find it so. My employer has come here expressly to talk to you.'

'I hope not professionally. I'm not now in business.'

'As head of the Security Executive? Everybody knows that, including my President. But retirement is an imprecise word and in your case it's been somewhat elastic.'

It was an irony and intended to be one. Also it stopped all argument. Both men shared an equal knowledge that Russell, since official retirement, had been more than once involved in affairs of state. Not always his own state's affairs at that.

The door opened and two men came in. There'd been no formal announcement, no hint of ceremony, but the ambassador's bow was rather lower than usual and his wife's gesture had been approaching a curtsy. 'Mr President,' the ambassador said.

The President came up to them, smiling. The other man stood against the wall, his eyes moving round the room in a single sweep. He was wearing a single-breasted dinner jacket and, since he kept the jacket open, Russell could see a wide silk cummerbund. But he didn't keep his weapon stuck in it.

Shoulder-holster, Charles Russell thought.

The three of them stood in a row and waited while the President made his greetings gracefully. Like Charles Russell he kissed his hostess's hand, saying something in very passable French; to his ambassador he used his own language, then he held out his hand to Russell.

'We meet again.'

Russell was taken aback but hid it. He knew the President's face from newspapers but to the best of his present recollection he had never met this man before. But the manners were too good for presumption so if he said they had met before they had. Russell waited for a clue in silence.

The President didn't seem offended. 'It was a long time ago,' he said with a smile. It wasn't a toothpaste smile like another's and he used it without affectation. 'Captain Smith, I recollect you called me, since my real name tied your tongue in knots. I suppose I should have been greatly offended but in fact I was very greatly flattered. I knew what you British thought of our army and 'Smith' somehow suggested I was really a soldier.'

Russell had it now and smiled in turn. It had indeed been some time ago. He'd had a difficult, even impossible job for 'Liaison' had been a dirty word and the officers detailed to practise its mysteries were seldom those of whom their regiments thought highly. But Russell had just had his second wound and somebody had to do the dirty work.

And it might, he remembered, have been very much dirtier, for this Captain had been no chocolate soldier. He came from a background of military incompetence unequalled since the Habsburg empire, but though he'd been too loyal to admit it Russell had been aware that he knew. Technically they'd been equals, liaising, but Smith had made it clear from the start that he'd be happy to take Captain Russell's orders. Suggestions if you insisted, then. They had got on together extremely well.

'Forgive me,' Charles Russell said.

'Not at all.'

'I remember you gave us some sound advice.' It was a slip and he would have liked to recall it. Admit that advice had once been accepted and you could reasonably be asked to return it politely. But that was water over the dam. Russell waited.

But the President didn't press his advantage; he was experienced and an excellent guest. 'We might talk about that later.'

'Of course.'

He began to speak of his visits to London. He came as a private citizen, these visits an unwelcome headache to Security, the police and the Home Office. He came because he liked a drink, for though he was privately far from pious, to drink in his own country would be unseemly. He came to buy his beautiful clothes, and it was rumoured for a change in his bed.

To Charles Russell all these were strong points in his favour. He had liked him once, now he liked him more. He watched the President's glass without seeming to. It was whisky, straight — his third, Russell thought. He was showing no visible sign whatever.

Yet another point in this pleasant man's favour.

The ambassador's wife had slipped away with an excuse about keeping an eye on the dinner and Russell had hidden an appreciative smile. He knew there was an excellent chef but his hostess was also a Frenchwoman.

Presently she came back and they all went in. It was a round table without formal precedence and the President sat on his hostess's right, Charles Russell at her other hand.

Next to Russell was the ambassador and beside him the ever-silent strongarm. As they sat down the President said:

'I once saved that man from a military lynching. Now he refuses to leave me — ever. He even insists on sleeping where I do. Often embarrassing, very embarrassing. But you won't find his table manners offensive and as you've guessed he speaks no human tongue.'

All of them knew good food when they saw it and none was inclined to insult a fine table by talking of any matter of moment. The President chatted to the ambassadress, switching from English to French with some fluency, and Russell talked golf to her husband quietly. Both had once been powerful strikers but both now complained that lack of length made golf a different and less interesting game.

The strongarm ate his food and stayed speechless.

They'd been waited on by a single manservant, evidently French too and expert. Cheese had come before the sweet, and now he put port wine on the table and a decanter of brandy beside the President. He bowed and withdrew and so did Her Excellency. Russell beat the President to the door of the room to open it wide for her.

When they were settled with drinks and cigars the ambassador tapped the table gently. 'Gentlemen,' he said, 'to business.'

It was Russell's private opinion they'd trapped him, but he hadn't improved his own position by an injudicious admission earlier and in any case he had eaten superbly. He couldn't just walk away so he'd listen.

The President began it smoothly. 'You know my position,' he said, 'but I'll state it. My country is in indifferent health and we can't afford another war. We have a bitter and traditional enemy but I'm convinced I could make a good peace with that enemy provided I could ditch those guerrillas. But I can't ditch the guerrillas; I do not dare. There's something which people call Arab opinion, and though generally it's about as futile as Resolutions in the United

Nations one arm of it works alarmingly well. I mean the oil barons to the east of me on whose handouts my country contrives to keep breathing. And those oil barons would be outraged if I opted out. Bang would go our subsidies, and war or no war we'd sink without trace.'

The President finished his brandy thoughtfully and the ambassador poured him another, his third. He'd had three or four whiskies and a bottle of wine, but he was still rock-steady and admirably lucid, a clear mind ticking away like a clock.

Charles Russell said nothing for he hadn't been asked to.

'The sting of it is that I don't like either of them, neither that murderous swaggering rabble nor the oil sheikhs whose puppet I am on a string.' The President snorted unexpectedly, a sound between contempt and hatred. 'The myth of the aristocratic Arab, the noble Bedu on his thoroughbred steed! In fact they're puritanical savages and they call me rude names behind my back. You can see that I'm not exactly pure Arab.'

Russell didn't comment but he could see. The thick curly hair, the flattish nose, were Hamitic before they were classical Arab. And the manner was very un-Arab too — none of an Arab's selfconscious *gravitas* but casual and friendly, even gay.

'You are wondering why I tell you all this since anyone with an interest in politics can read it between the lines in the newspapers? I tell you to define the boundaries, the limits of my freedom of action. For I've a smaller but also acuter problem, a neighbour who lives to the west, not the east. He's getting too big for his boots by far.'

'I agree he's an international nuisance.'

'Oil has gone to his head, already swollen. It isn't very high-class oil and it isn't going to last for ever, but he subsidizes way-out terrorists, he gets us a very bad name internationally, and on top of that he dreams dangerous dreams. He dreams about the renaissance of Araby. He doesn't yet dare to call himself Caliph but he likes to be called the Crown of the Faithful.' The President said it again in Arabic. Fastidiously he then used his handkerchief.

'You are asking for advice on this neighbour? You have diplomats better armed to give it.'

It was the tactful reply in a diplomat's presence but the ambassador promptly turned it aside.

'Diplomats may have information but the good ones will also admit that they're blinkered.'

The President said: 'I thank you, my friend.'

Charles Russell had known that he couldn't escape and now he was less than sure that he wished to. An interesting situation. He would have admitted that they'd hooked him neatly. He considered some time before he said :

'You are frightened of an invasion perhaps?'

The President laughed and so did Russell. The question had been a starter's gun, not a serious search for information. The President's army was still not a good one but it could make mincemeat of his immediate neighbour's.

Russell put out another feeler. 'You could always reverse it — invade yourself.'

This deliberate outrage was answered seriously. 'Indeed I could; I have often considered it. But the reason I gave you the lecture I did was to show that in matters of hard *realpolitik* I'm not the free fellow I'd like to be. I could take that wretched man over tomorrow but his oil would be far from compensation for the all-out sanctions brought against me. I don't mean the United Nations, I don't care a curse what they say or do, but sanctions by my brother Arabs. It would be seen as Cain and Abel again and I'd pay for it very dearly indeed. It might even trigger a third world war and I've nothing whatever to gain by that.'

'Then it's stalemate,' Russell said.

'It can't be.' The President finished his brandy, declined another; the President knew when to stop. His voice changed slightly and Russell noticed it. 'Outside this house is a bullet-proof car. I don't like driving in bullet-proof cars.'

'I didn't know your neighbour had gone for you.'

'Twice as it happens. Two too many.'

'You kept it remarkably quiet.'

'We had to. And quite apart from my personal safety there's organized, persistent subversion.'

'Serious?'

'I believe I can hold it. But I resent the fact that I'm forced to do so.'

Russell had let his cigar go out and he didn't often do that to a good one. 'Subversion,' he said reflectively.

'Yes?' The tone had been deliberately casual but Russell was much too experienced to be deceived by an affected innocence.

'Is a game which two can play quite happily. I believe you have many thousands of citizens working in that little man's country.'

'They're clerks and technicians. They're not trained men.'

'You could infiltrate. An eye for an eye.'

The President looked at his host and frowned. Some message had passed between them silently, something which Russell guessed was 'I told you so'. Unexpectedly both of them rose.

'I think we should join my wife at last.'

They went into the drawing-room and Madame gave them a second coffee. They talked socially of matters which interested them, the decay of the once great British theatre, how one couldn't buy a ticket nowadays without risking an evening of propaganda, how the rest of it was untidy trash or fit only for prurient adolescents, how *Seven Brides for Seven Brothers* had been resurrected again and was running strongly. Presently the President said:

'I'm sorry I must leave so early.' It was well past midnight and no one had noticed. 'I've an early plane to catch tomorrow.' He got up and kissed Madame's hand again.

'Will you be coming back for your parcels?'

'I will if I won't be intruding.'

'Of course not. And will you be wanting breakfast, please?' It had been delivered with a Gallic edge but the President returned it with interest.

'I believe it was the immortal Jorrocks who said that where he dined he slept. In my own case I prefer to take breakfast.' He added with almost Charles Russell's urbanity: 'However, one can never be sure.'

'Then just in case there'll be coffee and croissants.'

'That's really very kind indeed.'

In the hall the ambassador opened the door. The strong-arm went past to the car outside but Russell stopped at the door-jamb, staring incredulously. It was indeed a remarkable vehicle, something between an armoured car and a rather old-fashioned processional Daimler. The President saw his surprise and laughed.

'The provenance is equally interesting. It belonged to an S.S. General once, and at the end of the war, when the Reich was crumbling, he went off his head and had this built for him. One of my predecessors bought it for a song. I've a more modern one at home of course, since I never know when that tiresome man won't decide again I'm a suitable target, but this one I keep for my visits to London. I realize that a great many people would be much happier if I didn't make them but I'd go mad if I had to stay in my capital and visits of state were never my scene. May I offer you a lift, by the way?'

'I'd be fascinated,' Charles Russell said.

The guard was holding the door politely and when they were settled he climbed in to drive. He pressed the starter and after maybe four seconds the enormous engine coughed into life. 'Diesel,' the President said unnecessarily. 'Museum piece of its kind, they tell me. No acceleration whatever and maximum speed a steady fifty. But at fifty you could drive through a wall.'

They were out of Belgravia now, moving north, and the President looked at his watch and frowned. 'It's even later than I thought it was. Would you mind if we reversed the programme — I go first to my evident destination, then my man will drive you home without hurry? You'll have realized I mean to call on a lady, a tart or course, but a very high-class one, and it's unwise to keep a woman waiting. Midnight, I said, and it's well past that.

'I wouldn't mind at all. I'd enjoy the drive.'

It wasn't quite true for the car wasn't comfortable. The springing was unbelievably harsh, the engine was noisy, the gearbox more so. To change you had to double-declutch and sometimes the driver was less than perfect.

The President spoke to him and he nodded briefly. At Marble Arch they took the Edgware Road. Soon it was Maida Vale and they slowed to turn. Once to the left, once right, then left again. A quiet street of blocks of flats with porter's lodges.

The President spoke to the driver again and he began to draw into the kerb, braking heavily. As he slowed the first bullets hit the car, thudding against the armour plate.

'Drive on,' the President said, but uselessly. The front door had been pulled open violently and a hand had come in with a pistol and fired. The guard fell away from the wheel on the other seat. He balanced a moment, then slid to the floor. The door banged again, then total silence.

'A predicament,' the President said. His voice hadn't risen, he seemed quite calm. 'Unhappily I can't drive a car.'

Charles Russell didn't answer him for he was scrambling into the driver's seat. He had a poor opinion of Arab assassins but not so poor that he thought them fools. They must have known the car had armour: the gunfire had been designed to pin them down. So had been shooting the driver. Logical. They had halted and were an easy target. The next bang would not be the rattle of musketry but a missile with armour-piercing warhead. They could get such things without too much difficulty.

'Where are we going, Colonel?'

'Away from here.'

The dead driver had left the engine running and Russell,

for a dreadful moment, struggled to find first gear without finding it. At last it went in and he gunned the old engine. It roared in outraged protest but moved the car.

They had gone perhaps thirty or forty yards when there was a very much louder roar behind them. The blast caught them and rocked the car as he fought the wheel.

. . . I was wrong about the missile. A mine. They'd mined the road outside the lady's. Sensational — much better than simply shooting us sitting. How the bastards love a headline, damn them! We'd have gone up in the air like Mohammed's coffin and we wouldn't have come down alive.

The street had begun to fill with people, men in dressing-gowns, some angry, some frightened. At an open window a woman was screaming. Russell had stopped as the blast had caught them but now he drove on steadily, making west. In the silence before the pandemonium he'd heard something he knew and hadn't liked. The unmistakable wail of a police car's siren. Then something he had liked even less, gunfire again, quite heavy gunfire.

. . . Some very odd aliens live in this area so a patrol would be armed and they're shooting it out.

'Where are we going?' the President asked. He didn't seem frightened; he was cool as a sorbet.

'That's rather up to you, you know. You're not supposed to be here at all, far less to be involved in an incident.'

'I notice that we're going west.'

'To the west of us is a major airport.'

'You mean — '

'You make the propositions, please.'

The President started to think aloud. 'My country has an airline of sorts and I happen to be its Head of State. I ought to be able to fix it. Yes, I must.'

'If you can't get a passenger flight go as cargo. Anything which will get you out.'

'I agree with you but why are you helping me?'

Charles Russell said with cool acerbity: 'I'm not helping

you, I'm helping my country. There's going to be an appalling uproar — nobody can blanket this one — but if you're caught in this country there'll be worse than an uproar.'

'Security knows I've been here. I'm sure of it.'

'Of course it does but what of that? What matters to Security is the fact that you're alive and kicking. A President has been shot at and bombed but that President's been extremely considerate. Instead of staying where he'd be an embarassment he's withdrawn at once with a certain dignity.'

'It won't be dignified in a cargo hold. Apart from the fact that it may not be pressurized.'

'Up to you,' Russell said.

'Of course. I'll fix it.'

'A man in your position should do that.'

A hundred yards away from the Terminal Charles Russell brought the car to a halt. 'I'm afraid that a Head of State must walk the rest. I can't accept the outside chance that some porter would remember my face.'

The President nodded down at the body. 'And him?' he inquired. 'I was fond of him.'

'He'll be decently buried. I promise you that.'

'And the car?'

'I'll fix it, or at least I hope so. I'm going to need a ration of luck. So are you for that matter.' Russell held out his hand. 'God go with us both.'

'I'll remember this forever.'

'Forget it.'

'That I do not intend to do.'

Russell watched as the President started to walk, then turned the car and drove off deliberately. He had thought it all out and had weighed his chances. A car park would be out of the question, buying a ticket and exposing his face, and it was the sort of car which was easily memorable. Moreover it had a stiff on the floor. Then leave it on a ring road? Too chancy. That meant quite a walk back and that walk would be hazardous. Some airport policeman might intercept him and if he did he'd want explanations and good ones.

Charles Russell made his mind up quickly. A staff car park was the best bet open. At this time, at three o'clock in the morning, he doubted there'd be an attendant to check it.

He knew the airport well and drove to the nearest. There wasn't a soul in sight or moving. He wiped the wheel of the car with professional thoroughness and anywhere else where he thought he'd touched it.

He walked briskly back to the Central Terminal. A bus was just leaving, almost empty. He hesitated since that raised his risks, but a taxi would be out of the question. He bought his ticket and went on board.

The bus took him smoothly back to London.

Saliya was a grim little state, not so little if you counted its hinterland, bitter desert but a desert with oil. The rest was Mediterranean littoral, cultivable with skill and care but at the moment losing its battle against the sand. Many races had owned this uneasy country, Phoenicians, Hamites, Turks, all comers; and for a brief but to some men regretted period a wave of European colonizers. Now it was Arab again, or claimed so. It claimed it with a strident insistence, much too noisy for its neighbour the President, who was more concerned with the facts of real politics than talk of restoring the Arab world to a glory which he thought irrecoverable.

Ruling this curious state for the moment was the man they called the Crown of the Faithful. They did so not from sincere conviction but because he preferred that title himself and it was dangerous not to meet his wishes, more dangerous not to do so smiling. A few men would hide these smiles in their sleeves but all would smile because they must. It was true that he often backed dubious causes, splashing money about with the careless magnificence of a man who'd acquired it late in life and so hadn't been trained to use it with modesty. But his people were a conservative race and he'd done nothing to offend their prejudices. He hadn't usurped the title of Caliph, something which would have shocked the faithful since he couldn't claim descent from the Prophet in any of the recognized lines. He wasn't even an upper-class Arab but a young soldier with a subversive mind who had thrown out his Prince with barely a shot fired. This was the general opinion, then: it might have been very much worse under somebody else.

But he also had fanatical followers and Major Mahmud was the most devoted. He was close to his idol personally, a confidant knowing his secret plan. This was to master a neighbouring island, by financial infiltration at first and then by some sudden and crushing strike. After all it had once been Arab territory, then for centuries a fief of its Order. For a brief time French, then finally British. Now it had won its independence.

Mahmud smiled dryly: the word struck him as foolish. Nothing was free that wasn't viable — Saliya itself would collapse without oil — but the Island had nothing but a fierce xenophobia. The man who now ruled it played on that since he had very little else to play on. Not that he wasn't clever — he was. He wasn't called the Fox for nothing, not simply because he had flaming red hair.

But Mahmud was sure the Crown was cleverer. He had never accepted that lending money, that setting up the sort of company which gave work to the Island's teeming people, would be more than a process of softening-up. It had done exactly that and thoroughly.

So now it was going to be force or nothing, force at the right moment, naturally, when the preoccupations of greater Powers gave the use of it any real chance of success. But also the right sort of force.

The Crown of the Faithful had seen that too. He had an army and a General to run it and he'd chosen that General with proper care. He was a professional and perfectly safe; he was loyal and would never lead a *coup*; but equally he would kick like a camel if asked to lead an invasion across the sea. He'd protest that he didn't have that sort of army. Moreover this would be broadly true.

But not perfectly true and increasingly less so. Mahmud smiled again, this time happily. He was only a Major in formal rank since to promote him over the heads of others would have meant trouble with men a good deal senior, but in fact he held a Colonel's command. He was training two rather special regiments, not Maghrebi Arabs but desert Berbers. They were wiry and tough; they were nature's light infantrymen.

Nature's light infantrymen, nature's paratroops.

The General knew this but had shrugged resignedly. Militarily he was quietly orthodox, thinking paramen an unproven gimmick, but if the Crown of the Faithful wanted parachutists, parachute troops he must certainly have. In any case he held the purse-strings. The General was prepared to serve him but he hoped he could restrain his wild men. There were three Young Lions and Mahmud was one of them.

So Major Mahmud drove back from the training camp thoughtfully, calling in at his mosque for the evening prayer. He was a pious man as well as dedicated. His piety was in fact a reason for his blind faith in his unpredictable master. His master had an ideal, a dream, the resurgence of the Islamic world, and in that Arab culture had always been paramount. He followed and obeyed unquestioningly; he wouldn't have been ashamed to be called a slave.

He was thoughtful because he was also uneasy. The Crown was a very great man, he was sure of it, but he also had somewhat alarming habits. He hadn't offended Islamic opinion by usurping a title which most men held sacred, but although he didn't dare call himself Caliph he had modelled himself on one of the greatest. He wandered about at night unattended, talking to whomsoever he met; he was careless of security, his own and of more important matters; he had even been known to mislay state papers.

And that mistress of his. Major Mahmud frowned. He

took his own religion seriously, which meant he had little against Concerta's. There was nothing in Islamic law which forbade a man keeping a christian mistress; he could even marry a practising Christian and he wouldn't, for that alone, be damned. So it wasn't Concerta's faith which was troubling but the fact of her undeniable race. For Concerta was an Islander and Islanders were notoriously tricky.

Tricky and, much worse, revengeful. They would never forget a wrong nor forgive it.

And why had she stayed behind when the others had gone? All the Islanders had gone but a handful. They'd owned farms and property, running both profitably, but the Crown had sent them bundling home with the Italians who had owned even more. The farms were running downhill fast, producing a third of what they had, but this wasn't a matter the Crown thought important. Land belongs to him who uses it best? That wasn't a dictum the Crown agreed with. He wanted it back in Arab hands and if that meant it slowly went back to desert that was better than the standing offence of seeing it in alien hands. Besides, he could always import his food. Oil would pay for it and leave plenty to spare.

Concerta's father had been one of these colonists, tri-lingual in his own harsh tongue, in Maghrebi Arabic, even Italian. He had owned perhaps five hundred hectares, not all of it rich but all well farmed, some property too, a row of shops. Now the land had gone and the family with it. All except Concerta who had stayed. She had stayed in one of the shops and still ran it; she'd been allowed to because she provided a service. She was in fact the best butcher in town with a clientèle which had included the Crown when he'd been only a very junior officer with a secret plan to lead a rebellion. She stood behind the counter and butchered herself.

Major Mahmud permitted something near to a grin. Nature had well endowed her to do so. She was a biggish woman, still handsome at forty, with fine breasts and even finer forearms. The cleaver came down with a confident whack, the knife trimmed the fat off, and there you were. Major Mahmud, like most other Arabs, preferred a woman to look like a woman. He could well understand why his master had taken her but he nevertheless deplored his choice. She was an alien with a suspect background. She might even be one of the Fox's spies.

The Major's grin had disappeared for he was seeing a difficult duty ahead of him. He was as close to the Crown of the Faithful as any man and once he had raised the matter bluntly. . . . Was it really wise, was it even sensible, to keep as a mistress an ex-colonial?

The Crown had promptly bitten his head off.

And now Mahmud felt he must speak again. The liaison was too dangerous in principle, and where he saw a plain duty Major Mahmud would follow it.

2

Charles Russell had spent an anxious ten days, for the scandal had been loud and immediate. The headlines had flamed in furious anger — ANOTHER ARAB OUTRAGE IN LONDON — and the more serious papers had frankly been frightened. Must London become a mid-Eastern battlefield, factions for whom its people cared nothing shooting it out in its shabby streets? It was time that the government acted firmly.

No paper suggested what firm action.

Russell had thought it over carefully. The area where the attack had been made was thickly seeded with suspect aliens and two incidents had already occurred there. It hadn't been coincidence that a patrol car had been prowling circumspectly, and it was just as well that in fact it had. The attackers must surely have brought their own transport and when the mine failed they'd have used it to follow. That old bullet-proof monster was short on speed and sooner or later they'd have caught and blocked her. When Charles Russell and Mr friendly President would have had no chance worth an outside bet; they'd either have had to get out or to take it, and taking it would have meant more than a peppering. The car's armour was proof against fire from small arms but Russell couldn't believe that they'd only had that. It was clear the attack had been carefully planned and all careful plans had a second leg to them. The small-arms fire had been used to halt them but if the blast of the mine hadn't killed them messily there'd have been something much more potent and messier.

The Arab assassin, he thought again. He loved killing because it was in his blood but even more he loved his two-inch headlines.

Instead they had let them go and shot it out. Russell couldn't withhold a mild admiration. In any sort of battle formation Arabs were the worst soldiers on earth, but in the arts of ambush they didn't lack courage and they did have a pride and a certain arrogance. So they'd chosen to stand and fight it out with a patrol they must have guessed was armed. Since this wasn't an ambush they'd bought it badly. A policeman had been severely wounded but all three Arabs had fallen together.

That was one thing on the plus side, certainly: nobody living and therefore no trial. But a formal Inquiry had started already and Charles Russell did not desire a subpoena. He wanted to go on living quietly and in any case he was due for a holiday. He wanted to keep out of this for his name was still well known where it mattered and the part he had played had been more than equivocal.

Well, who knew he'd been there? Just one living man and that was the President. But the President had no need to involve him and the motive of gratitude not to do so. With any sort of reasonable luck he'd have given his ambassador orders. They'd have come in one of the higher ciphers and the ambassador would obey them unquestioningly. No doubt the Foreign Office would ask him to call since if he chose he could decline the police and protocol was a sacred cow. He might even be seen by the Foreign Secretary, but that was so much the better: the man was a lightweight. He was a faintly rodent-like intellectual, long on ambition but short on sense. The ambassador would twist him three ways. Russell smiled as he saw the imagined scene.

'Good morning, Your Excellency.'

'Good morning, Minister.'

Won't you sit down?'

H.E. would have done so, crossing his legs. His legs were longer than his race's average; he was proud of them and wore beautiful trousers. So he'd sit silently and wait for the gambit.

'This is a very awkward affair.'

The ambassador sighed though no sound escaped him. This wasn't an opening, simply a fluff. This conceited young man was inexperienced. The ambassador would have much preferred a discreet little chat with a senior official. So the first real move must come from himself.

'Mr President is back in our country. He has already appeared on a public occasion. I understand that he's in excellent health.'

'A policeman is not and three Arabs are dead.'

'It's improbable that they're also my countrymen.'

The Foreign Secretary frowned. It was designed to make his sharp face more weighty but in fact it simply made him look irritable. 'I suggest that we come to the point.'

'By all means. I will answer any questions I can.'

'Your Excellency is exceedingly kind.' It was intended as an elegant irony but came over as a schoolboy sarcasm. The ambassador ignored it politely. As a professional he thought the man corny.

'Perhaps you will let me guess your first question. Who was present at my house that evening? Myself and my wife and of course the President. The President brought his Man Friday with him. The only other guest was a Colonel Russell.'

'Colonel Charles Russell?'

'Yes, that's the man.'

'Colonel Russell is a retired official.'

'I doubt if he'd choose that word himself but he ran your Security Executive brilliantly.'

'A rather strange guest at an embassy party.'

'No, not at all, we're quite old friends. We've played golf together more than once and we happen to have a club in common.' A pause, then the ambassador added: 'I also understand that he knows my wife. And it wasn't an embassy party in any sense. It was a gathering of civilized adults' — a sharp and biting edge to this — 'whose company I find congenial.'

'But your President was there.'

'Indeed. I said they were people I find congenial and the President is a friend of mine quite apart from the fact that he also employs me.'

'His incognito visits cause a great deal of trouble.'

'That I'm obliged to deny officially. He comes here for clothes and other matters and has always been very discreet indeed.' The ambassador switched from defence to attack; he was a professional and a very good one. 'You cannot lay it at my President's door that hoodlums attack him in the streets of your capital.'

The Foreign Secretary knew he'd been neatly wrong-footed so he didn't reply to this but pondered. He had a special face for this and he put it on. Finally he came to the point. 'It's Russell that really worries me.'

'Why?'

'I should have thought that would be perfectly obvious.' This time it was an open sarcasm, naked to the point of insult. His Excellency showed no sign of resenting it. If this conceited little man had no manners it wasn't his business to teach him propriety.

'Not to me,' he said smoothly. 'Russell wasn't with the President, or not when the attack was made. The President offered a lift — to drop him off. I heard him do it and Russell accepted. If you care to look at a map that was natural. Russell's flat is only a bare half mile from the route to the President's assignation.'

The image faded to be replaced by another. The ambassador had taken his leave and the most senior of all officials sat in his place. 'Russell,' the Foreign Secretary said again.

'I think I follow your thought — yes, I'm sure of it. He's a man with a certain aura, isn't he? He never plays on it but he can never escape it.'

'We can't hide that he went to that wretched dinner party. The Americans won't like that at all. They're playing for very high stakes with that President. They might think we were trying to cut in on their table.'

'They might well think that but we cannot prevent it. So Charles Russell went to a private party and there he met an eminent statesman. That is water under the bridge. It's happened.'

The Foreign Secretary thought for some time, then said: 'There's something about this affair which smells.'

The official kept his face impassive. This man boasted of his intuitions. Unhappily they were mostly wrong.

'You are thinking of what happened afterwards — the President's flight, the abandoned car, complete, as it happened with inconvenient corpse? The police have looked into that of course, but I've always found the police to be sensible. All sensible men have a simple rule which is to take the very simplest hypothesis which will cover all the facts as they're known, and in this case that is simple indeed.' The official relit his ritual pipe. 'Then there were more than three terrorists and more than one car. The three who chose to fight it out didn't do so for a love of fighting but to cover the escape of the others. And more than merely craven escape. When the mine failed to kill the President cleanly they followed him to Heathrow to try again. Somehow he got away but his bodyguard didn't. They found him misparking the armoured car and they shot him dead to keep his mouth shut. I can tell you it was a well-organized job. The car had been wiped as clean as a whistle.'

'I don't like it,' the Foreign Secretary said.

'May I ask what you don't like?' It was curt. The official was a busy man, too busy for adolescent hunches.

'I don't like Russell.'

'What aspect of Russell?'

'Suppose, just suppose, he had something to do with it. Suppose he had some private knowledge making nonsense of the police hypothesis.'

'Since you ask me to suppose I will.'

'What would he do if the police asked him questions? I imagine he'd tell a pack of lies.'

'Have you ever met him?"

'No.'

'If you had you wouldn't ask the question. Apart from any question of principle he's far too experienced to lie to the police. When you do so the odds are stacked against you and Charles Russell is a man who plays them. I've played bridge with him to my cost and know.'

There was a silence, then the Minister said: 'I don't want Charles Russell before that Inquiry. I don't want him brought on stage at all.' The Minister's voice was normally loud, almost an orator's boom, and confident. Now it had shrunk to almost nothing.

'I think I understand you, Minister.'

'Could you convey my preference?'

'Certainly.'

Charles Russell woke from his reverie sharply, walking across the room to a calendar. It was ten days since he'd helped an embarrassed President and the Inquiry had been sitting for six. He hadn't been called to attend its proceedings and if the police had an interest they hadn't disclosed it, neither some very senior officer with a murmur about having luncheon somewhere nor a polite young man who would ring the doorbell. Russell decided they weren't going to bother him. After all they had powerful motive not to.

Which meant he could take his holiday after all. He'd been considering a month in Majorca, an island which, though exploited brutally, still offered superlative swimming and sometimes sun. But his morning mail made him reconsider for it had brought him a letter from Robert Mortimer. Robert had married and settled down on another island — no, *The* Island. The Press had begun to call it that since it was sneaking into the news quite often. Not the headline news beloved of terrorists but on pages four and five where the real meat lay. And here was an invitation to visit it, one from his ex-Chief Assistant.

Surprising, Russell thought, but agreeable. It was eight years since he had last seen Mortimer, and their parting, though perfectly friendly, had been abrupt. Mortimer had simply walked in one day and offered Russell his resignation.

Charles Russell hadn't blamed him for that; he couldn't since he'd have done the same. For Mortimer had been good at his job, the natural heir to Russell's chair as head of the Security Executive, and Russell, as his retirement drew closer, had even proposed the succession discreetly. But at once they had turned it down and Russell knew why. Mortimer had one fatal defect which was political views which he didn't hide. They weren't so different from Russell's own, but Russell had the steely discipline to conceal that he had views at all. In Whitehall and its more interesting environs the road to a steady promotion was clearly marked. It was as fatal under any government to be known as a crusading socialist as it was to wear a swastika in your hat. The accepted and therefore the gainful aura was one of a sort of half-baked humanism. Provided you worked like a patient donkey, letting your private life rot miserably, you'd rise at least to Assistant Secretary. Any Minister, whether of Left or Right, preferred to be served by faceless neuters.

Charles Russell had recommended Mortimer but he'd known in his heart that he wouldn't succeed him. The penny had dropped with Mortimer too, so he'd walked in one morning, walked out a month later. It had been clean and decisive and entirely impersonal, they had parted without a hint of ill-feeling, but since then Charles Russell had only had Christmas cards. They hadn't met once nor proposed a meeting.

Natural enough, Charles Russell reflected, since Mortimer was now on the Island and the Island meant maybe three hours' flying. But his choice had greatly surprised his late master. Mortimer had been in the prime of life, an active man with an active mind, and here he was stuck in the Med, on an Island, married to an Islander with three sons and possibly more to come. They were notably a prolific people. But he hadn't been forced to make that choice, he wasn't some broken-down badly paid pensioner obliged by health or perhaps by poverty to live where he didn't wish to settle. Robert Mortimer had been comfortably off.

Russell looked at the letter again and hesitated. He was tempted but there were also drawbacks. For he'd been to the Island and hadn't much cared for it. He'd been once in the war though he hadn't intended it and once before and that had offended him. The place had been a suburb of Portsmouth and Portsmouth wasn't his favourite city. Rich Navy playing noisy polo, poor Navy calling on Admirals assiduously. And they hadn't treated the Islanders handsomely.

Nobody had treated them handsomely. Look at that preposterous Order. Its member might have had sixteen quarterings (the Germans had wanted thirty-two) and they were certainly clean of base blood or Jewish, but Russell didn't consider them honourable. They'd been allowed to withdraw from defeat on a promise, the promise they'd never fight Islam again, and within two years and some said less their galleys were scourging the Mediterranean. They had once been stout-hearted fighting men who had stood off a famous siege with glory, but in the end they had decayed in shame. The last Master had simply given in, removing himself not with bang but with whimper. Now they had a house in Rome, insisting with a tiresome emphasis that their status was still a Sovereign Order whilst their name and original *raison d'être* had been coolly usurped in a protestant country.

They had had their undoubted moments of glory, but who had made that glory possible? The Islanders, Russell had long since decided, the Islanders whom they had treated despitefully. The Islanders hadn't borne arms? What rubbish! What pompous, heraldic, medieval rubbish. The Islanders had borne arms with distinction. They might have been serfs of a foreign Order but they were the best artillerymen in the Mediterranean. One salvo had normally been enough for few Barbary pirates would face a second. And in the latest of wars they'd revived that tradition. The crews of anti-aircraft guns had fallen around their weapons still firing, but if the gun had not been destroyed entirely another crew would come in singing, as often as not with its parish priest. Or take away a couple of centuries, nothing in the Island's long history, when the French had been expelled ignominiously. (Everybody, the British included, seemed to leave the Island with less than dignity.) They had ruled a few years with a Gallic arrogance which had made the old Order look mild in comparison, but it hadn't been only the British blockade and the landing of a handful of soldiers which had bundled out the French in defeat; there'd been a genuine insurrection internally, men pressed too far and dark deeds done.

For they weren't naturally a subservient people; they were spiky and proud, above all things revengeful. It was very unwise to do them an injury. Once Russell had given offence unintentionally and the blow had followed at once, on a reflex. There were people who contrived to love them but what Russell felt was a real respect.

For the third time he looked at Mortimer's letter. Things had changed on the Island and changed for the better. The Fox was a thorn in several sides, almost as sharp as his unfortunate predecessor, but his people were walking their earth with their heads up. If Russell had been an Islander he'd have voted for the Fox unhesitatingly.

He went to the telephone, ringing his travel agent, then sent Mortimer a grateful telegram.

Major Mahmud was walking to see his master, conscious of a difficult duty, a story to tell which he thought was ominous; and he must tell it himself or not at all. There was nothing in the state of Saliya which could properly be called a cabinet: coterie was a better word, a coterie of devoted admirers. Mahmud was one of three of these and Suleiman ran the Crown's Intelligence. With another they were called the Young Lions.

And Suleiman had just had bad news. It was unseemly that the Crown of the Faithful should be keeping a female butcher as mistress. It was intolerable when she was also a spy.

The Crown was an irascible man so they'd tossed up who should tell him. Mahmud had lost.

Now he was on his way, heavy-hearted. There was a broken-down palace but the Crown didn't use it.He lived in a modest surburban villa guarded by a single soldier. Who saluted Major Mahmud creditably, but he knew him and he didn't challenge. Mahmud went straight upstairs and knocked.

'Come in whoever you are.'

Mahmud frowned. It had been typical of his master's insouciance and Mahmud thought he overdid it. He went in and waited.

'Please sit down. I imagine you're going to ask for money, in which case you shall have what you need. But I thought the latest toy was those helicopters.'

'It isn't money this time.'

'Then tell me what.'

'It's very bad news.'

'Then tell it quickly.'

Major Mahmud had decided his line. It would be better to blurt it out and accept the recoil. 'That woman Concerta. She is also a spy.'

The expected explosion did not follow. The Crown was in a rare mood of placidity. 'How do you know?' he asked indifferently.

Mahmud told the alarming facts. 'She has a sister who went back to the Island, where she settled down and married an Englishman. That we have always known, of course. What we didn't know till that damned Greek discovered it was that her husband works in the Fox's Intelligence.

The damned Greek was their chief ear on the Island.

'Which makes her a spy?'

'It doesn't prove it. But the evidence suggests — '

'It does not.' The Crown was emphatic but still perfectly reasonable. 'You think she's the Fox's agent?'

'She could be.'

'I'm afraid I consider that very loose thinking. What could she hope to gain from my company?'

Mahmud thought it wise not to answer. The Crown was notoriously careless with papers and men said foolish things in bed. The Crown noticed the silence but didn't resent it; he was still in an unexplained good temper.

'She was brought here as a child and has stayed. A trip or two back to the Island perhaps, but no doubt you have already checked that she has never left this country for long.' He leant forward to make his point the clearer. 'Where did she get her training, then?'

'Training?'

'That's what I said and that's what I meant. The Fox isn't given that name for nothing and I don't think he'd use an untrained agent. Especially an untrained woman agent.'

Mahmud hadn't thought of that, nor had his colleague, the man of Intelligence. But he was stubborn and was facing a duty; he said at length:

'May I speak freely?'

'I can't stop you but I can guess what you're thinking. You're thinking I may have blabbed in bed.' This was too true to be worth an answer and the Crown of the Faithful continued easily. 'I haven't but suppose I did. Suppose I even told her in terms that we plan to take her Island over. Would that matter so much?'

'I'd have thought a great deal.'

'And again I think you're thinking loosely. The Fox must

know or at least suspect it. So does everyone else with a knowledge of politics. Every diplomat in the eastern Med has been reporting it to his masters for months. Not the details, I hope, not those regiments you're training, but the intention, no, the probability, must be as clear as though we'd sent out a circular. Why are we pouring in money daily, backing industries we know aren't viable? Why, in short, do we keep them from starving? There's no love lost between us, there never has been. It wouldn't matter much to us if their whole silly sham collapsed tomorrow. Unless, that is, we'd a *practical* interest. Unless, that is, what we meant to inherit was a going concern and not a ruin.'

'I hadn't seen it that way.'

'Try to.'

The Crown sent for coffee for two and they drank it. He was relaxed but now he relaxed some more. 'In any case you needn't worry. It's high time I married again and got sons.'

Major Mahmud nodded; he thought this praiseworthy. He hadn't any interest in women — they were there to bear sons, not for serious pleasure — but the Crown's first wife had died in childbirth when he'd still been an unknown junior officer. Since then he had come to power and had used it, but he'd also been a busy man. The private disciplines of a formal marriage had been something he hadn't had time to assume.

They were talking as friends, not disciple and master, and Mahmud asked the obvious question.

'What about Concerta?'

'What of her?'

'She isn't going to take it kindly.'

'She'll have no chance to take it otherwise.'

Major Mahmud stared but said nothing. It struck him as entirely unscrupulous but his master was an unscrupulous man. He wouldn't have got where he was if he hadn't been.

But the Crown saw his face and laughed, unoffended. 'I'm afraid you've got it wrong again. I'm not going to have her killed — just get rid of her. I don't want her hanging around in Saliya, spreading gossip and maybe trying to make trouble. So I'm sending her back to her Island.'

'How are you going to do that?'

'Shut her shop.'

'What's she going to do then?'

'I can see you don't know her. She'll go straight to her bank and inquire of her balance. Where I hope she will get a most pleasant surprise.' He added without a muscle moving: 'It isn't seemly to throw out a woman penniless.'

'But she won't be able to take it out.'

'Oh yes she will. I've fixed all that.'

'You seem to have thought of everything.'

'Yes.' This wasn't true, he'd missed something important. Concerta was an Islander, which wasn't a race to take insult mildly.

Major Mahmud walked back to his lodging contented. He thought he'd come out of the evening well. He was dedicated but he wasn't clever. These were signal defects but not necessarily fatal. Unhappily he added a third. He was as stubborn as the proverbial mule.

Charles Russell had had an agreeable flight but at the airport it was less agreeable. They were rebuilding it to cope with the tourists and the place was unashamedly chaos. He didn't blame them for that, Heathrow could be worse, but his cabin bag had been rather heavy and he'd been obliged to walk with it half a mile. There'd been porters but only for first-class passengers and Russell seldom travelled first class on any journey which was less than four hours. He arrived at the Terminal hot, with his arms aching, and stood in a sweating queue with his passport. The girl stamping them was very slow with that manner of piggish I'm the Boss which minor officials affected everywhere. It was going to take an hour to get cleared.

But it didn't for a man tapped his shoulder. 'Colonel Charles Russell?'

'I am.'

'Please come with me.'

They went through a door at the side of the queue to a neat little office with a desk and two chairs. The official waved at one of them. 'Please sit down.' Russell took it, the official the other. The desk was between them, authority's symbol. 'Your passport, please.'

Russell handed it over and the official flicked through it. 'Your photograph tallies,' he said at length.

'May I ask with what.'

'With the one in our records.'

Charles Russell was annoyed but not surprised. This wasn't the first time he'd been taken from passport queues. It was a nuisance and entirely unjustified but it was something he had learned to live with.

'The purpose of your visit, Colonel?'

'I'm a tourist. I'm going to stay with a friend.'

'Have you been to the Island before?'

'Yes, twice. Once was in the war and doesn't count.'

'Why doesn't that count?'

'Because I was then a serving soldier. My ship was bombed and I had to swim for it. As it happened I only just made it.'

. . . Only just.

'And the other time?'

'That was earlier, I was only a boy. I came to stay with a distant relation.'

'May I know his name?'

Charles Russell gave it.

'But that man was the Governor.'

'Yes, he was. He was also a very distant cousin being kind to a boy who needed a holiday.'

'I see,' the official said. 'I see.'

. . . He thinks I'm some nostalgic imperialist coming back to gloat on the natives' balls-up. Difficult to blame him, really. There are such people still, quite a few of them.

But the official had recovered his manners. 'I must ask you a formal question, sir. You would find that to mislead me would be unwise. Your sole purpose on this Island is tourism? I emphasize the "sole" and intend to.'

'I don't mean to work here if that's what you mean.'

'It is not what I meant and I think you know it.'

'I'm no longer a political animal.'

'That isn't entirely your reputation.'

'My reputation is greatly exaggerated. Often, as now, it's a source of annoyance.'

'To us it might be more than annoying.'

'Can you think of any way I could use it?'

'Frankly, no.'

'Then I hope you will permit me to land.'

'After one more tiresome question, sir. You said you were going to stay with a friend. I'd like to know his name if I may.'

'Robert Mortimer,' Charles Russell said.

The manner changed again sensationally. 'Major Robert Mortimer?'

'I doubt if he calls himself Major now.'

'You should have told me this before.'

'You didn't ask.'

The official stamped Russell's passport and held it out. 'My apologies, sir,' he said.

'For doing your duty? None are necessary.'

The official was on his feet and smiling. 'Is Major Mortimer meeting you?'

'Yes, he is.'

'He has a car outside?'

'I imagine he has.'

'Then permit me to escort you to it.'

'That's kind of you but I've had a long journey. I'd like to wash my hands and freshen up.'

But he didn't go to freshen up; he went into the hall to think. Mortimer could wait a minute and he wanted to clear his head before meeting him. He'd been grilled at airports before and knew the form. This one had run notably wide of it. It had started as they always did with an official who held the whip and knew it, then changed to an open and cold hostility at the mention of a harmless Governor long since in his grave and wholly forgotten. But not, it seemed, forgotten here. And the moment he'd given Mortimer's name hostility had changed to obsequiousness. That needed some sort of explanation and at the moment he couldn't make even a guess. He knew that the Island was oddly run but surely not as oddly as this. You didn't need a lifetime's experience to smell that there was something unusual and whatever that was hung round Mortimer's neck.

Now he'd have to go and join him and something was in the air he didn't like.

3

Charles Russell woke next morning early. The journey and the scene at the airport had taken more from him than once they would have, but the Mortimers had been more than considerate. Mortimer had presented his wife, Lucia, and three little boys in well-pressed shorts who had stood in a line with their hands behind them. When spoken to they had come to attention, for the Island, though it was changing fast, was still a long way from a permissive society. Then the Mortimers had served a light supper and packed Russell off to his bed with their blessing.

Russell looked at his watch: it was half past six. A little early for tea but they'd told him to ring for it, so he pressed the bell and waited hopefully. Almost at once a maid appeared, smiling. She had the typical powerful shoulders and forearms of any Mediterranean woman and her hair was done in a modest chignon.

'Good morning,' Russell said.

'Good morning, sir. I'm sorry I don't speak English proper.'

'You speak it well enough for me.'

'You are nice,' she said. The word amused him.

'I could be nicer if you brought me some tea.'

She bobbed and departed and came back with the tea. Russell propped himself up on a couple of pillows, trying to adjust to the unexpected.

For Robert Mortimer was living in style. The car which

he had brought to the airport had been an unpretentious family runabout but his house had surprised Charles Russell considerably. He had expected some standardized villa or bungalow in an area where retired folk settled, but had found instead a fine stone house in a quarter which he remembered as opulent. Today it said 'diplomats' or 'especially rich tourists' and Mortimer was emphatically neither. Robert Mortimer hadn't been poor by some distance but this establishment had come as a shock. It wasn't extravagant since neither was Mortimer, but they'd been waited on by an elderly manservant. He'd worn an ordinary black suit to do so but also white cotton gloves to serve them, and in such small talk as his hosts had allowed before Russell had been dismissed to his bed Robert Mortimer had mentioned the children. They would soon have to go to England for schooling and that was going to cost the earth. He had spoken with some apprehension but also with the quiet resignation of a man who when pressed could somehow find money. Charles Russell decided he'd started some business, or perhaps an aged aunt had died, leaving him much more than expected. He had the sort of background where such things still happened.

Russell shaved and bathed and went down to breakfast. His hosts were before him and already at table, but there wasn't any sign of the children. No doubt there was a nursery and possibly a Scottish nanny. They exchanged Good Mornings and Robert waved at the sideboard.

'Help yourself to what you fancy.'

Normally Russell didn't eat breakfast unless he were playing golf in the morning, but supper had been very light and the sideboard looked extremely tempting. There were sausages and eggs and bacon, kedgeree and a dish of grilled kidneys, almost an Edwardian competence. Russell chose kedgeree and sat down to eat it. Mortimer had had eggs and bacon and, Russell suspected, a couple of sausages. Now he was on to toast and marmalade. He had always been a notable trencherman.

Lucia said: 'Robert! You're going to get fat.' She said it with a certain envy for she was a type which had to watch its weight. But Robert could eat what he liked and did, and Robert's waist would still stay tidy. He was in fact as slim as a model.

'Nonsense, my dear — you're talking nonsense and know it. The day I get fat you can find somebody else.'

She laughed and shrugged and gave him best. They were evidently on excellent terms.

Robert poured a last cup of the excellent coffee. 'There's nothing that needs doing this morning. Would you care to come shopping?'

'I'd like that very much.'

'So be it. We can natter while the women work. And bring an unbrella. I smell the rain.'

Charles Russell hadn't brought an umbrella but Mortimer found a spare and lent it. On the steps of the house they were joined by the cook, a stout smiling woman who held out her hand.

. . . That wouldn't have happened ten years ago.

They went down the steps and across the road. On the other side was a creek of the harbour, a small marina with boats of all kinds from flashy cabin cruisers to launches. Mortimer's was something between, a motorboat with a retractable awning. There was a popple on the water already and a man at the boat's stern awaiting them. He greeted them without subservience and Mortimer spoke in the boatman's tongue. Lucia, who had excellent manners, translated as he did so easily.

'He's asking whether it's safe to go.'

'And what's the answer?'

'George says it's safe to go all right but we may have to take a taxi back.'

She might have added but thought it wiser not to that Robert usually sailed alone. But this morning the boatman was coming too. He was insisting on that and Robert agreeing.

They climbed in the boat and Robert started the engine. In the creek the water was smooth enough but as they crossed a neck of the harbour they started to pitch. It was nothing worse than a mild discomfort and Mortimer stayed at the helm till they landed. It had begun to rain but the awning sheltered them. The boatman was looking up at the sky.

They tied up at a yacht club and climbed a staircase. The women went about their mysteries and Mortimer led the way to a café. 'Brandy?' he inquired. 'It's quite good. Not a *fine* of course, but it's perfectly potable. All the drinks here have improved enormously.'

Russell had already noticed it. The wine the evening before had been admirable.

Over the brandy Robert Mortimer talked. 'You like my adopted Island?'

'I've only been here for a matter of hours.'

'You will find it very greatly changed. I genuinely like the people and I don't say that because I married one. They have characteristics I quietly deplore but I like to see them walking upright and they haven't done that for several centuries. That Order of theirs and then ourselves. . . .' He left it unfinished and drank some more brandy. 'The Fox is not the late Prime Minister — he's backpedalling on most of his policies — but he hasn't changed our methods of government.'

'Some of them seem a little unorthodox.'

'Unorthodox!' Robert Mortimer laughed. 'You still have your taste for understatement. There are countries where Trade Unions demonstrate but few where they take to the streets in force at the express behest of their own Chief Executive. It isn't a formal dictatorship yet, there's still an opposition party, but all it can do is bewail the past.'

'From what I know of the Island, which isn't much, your Fox has a pretty thin majority.'

'And I know of men who would like to change sides. They don't do so because they do not dare.' He held up a hand to silence Russell. 'No, I don't mean they'd be gunned down in the streets nor tried on some trumped-up charge and imprisoned. But our crowds have a habit of turning violent, houses have been known to burn, and a yacht or two has disappeared.' He added without changing his manner: 'The Med can be very treacherous water.'

They were back again on the old terms of intimacy and Russell asked:

'I gather you have work here.'

'Yes. I run a sort of business. Quite lucrative.'

'I rejoice for you, but isn't it difficult?'

'It would be if I had no protection.'

Charles Russell considered another question, wondering how to ask it discreetly, but the women had returned with their baskets. They went back down the stairs to the waiting boat. The rain had stopped but the wind was stronger. The boatman spread his hands and shook his head. It was the international gesture for No Go.

Robert Mortimer frowned. 'We've a guest for luncheon. A taxi will take us very much longer.'

'Better do as George says, dear.'

'No, it's only a blow. And it isn't as though you were seasick, either.'

Mortimer, Russell knew, could be stubborn. He was leading the way and had passed the boatman. Charles Russell saw his wife raise her eyebrows. The boatman shook his head resignedly.

In the harbour it was rough but tolerable. The cook was retching miserably, calling on the Madonna and Saints, but apart from that there was nothing disturbing. They motored across the neck of the harbour, shipping a little water but not a lot. Russell noticed the boat had a good deal of freeboard.

But in the creek the sudden storm caught them savagely, brutal and entirely terrifying, the eye of a Mediterranean squall. The awning had gone in a second to nowhere, the rain came down in remorseless sheets. What had once been a creek was now a whirlpool. The lightning glittered, the thunder snarled. Against the fine old buildings which stood back from the quay it was the backdrop to some Wagnerian extravagance.

The boatman took the tiller from Mortimer, turning the boat's head to the wind and waiting. He said something in his own strange language and this time Mortimer did the translation.

'He says we can ride it out with luck. But if the engine goes we've had it properly.'

'Why should the engine go?'

'From the water. We're shipping quite a lot already.'

It was true, they were shipping the crests of the waves. In the cockpit it was ankle deep. Lucia was telling her beads in silence but the cook was in hysteria openly.

Russell looked at the shore — fifty yards at most. He could make that in any sea on earth. Mortimer, he knew, could swim, but he knew nothing of his wife in rough water. The boatman was a bit of a toss-up for Russell had heard of fine seamen who couldn't swim. The cook? Even if she could swim she would panic.

Suddenly the big one caught them, shipping it green in a solid wall. Now it was knee high, not ankle. The engine coughed twice, then petered out. The wind began to move them across the waves.

'The next one's going to turn us over.'

It did exactly that. They were all in the sea.

Charles Russell looked around him calmly; he was totally at home in water. Robert Mortimer was towing his wife. The cook he couldn't see at all and he wriggled out of his coat and shoes. He dived for her and didn't find her, but when he came up for air she had surfaced too. She was thrashing about and shouting noisily and Russell got behind to help her. As he'd rather suspected she fought him bitterly. Reluctantly he hit her hard, then he started to pull her back to the shore.

When he got there his hosts had arrived before him. They

stretched the cook out and began to pump her, but in fact she was a long way from drowning. She hiccuped twice and got to her knees, then finally to her feet and upright. Charles Russell thought it characteristic that she offered no single word of thanks. Instead she said:

'I must see about lunch. We've lost what we bought but I'll manage somehow.'

She began to stump off to the house quite steadily.

'They're a very tough lot,' Charles Russell said.

'They are indeed.' Robert Mortimer pointed. The boatman was still with the boat, hanging on to it. The squall was abating but there he was.

'Can't he swim?'

'Like a fish.'

'Then what's he still doing there?'

'He took the tiller and that made him captain.'

Charles Russell thought this romantic rubbish. 'But aren't you going to get him in?'

'Of course I am, I'll do it now.' Another man had already approached them. There was a brief exchange which went over Charles Russell but it seemed to be some sort of haggle. Finally Mortimer shook the man's hand. 'He wants six pounds in Island money. Considering there's still quite a wind I consider that perfectly fair and reasonable.'

'And your boat?'

'She will probably sink but we'll get her up. There's a floating crane for this sort of incident. It's expensive but also extremely efficient.' He was as cool as though he'd been walking down Regent Street. 'Now let's get back and change our clothes.'

As they went up the steps Charles Russell said sideways: 'I suppose that little blow was genuine. You did speak of yachts which disappeared.'

'The Fox can't control the elements yet, though if he could he might have laid that on for you. There were lessons to be learnt from it.'

'Yes?'

'We're hardy as well as rash and emotional. But I think you've realized that already. So secondly we survive quite beautifully. On this Island very alarming things happen — anywhere else they'd be plain disasters — but when the storm is over we're very much here still.'

Russell went up to his room and changed. He had brought a bottle of whisky with him and he poured three generous fingers and drank it. He went down to the sitting-room but Robert Mortimer had outpaced him.

'Are you all right?'

'I hope to survive.'

'I'm glad because we've a guest for luncheon. He talks too much but he talks very well. He's a priest, by the way, but I don't think you mind them.'

'Why should I mind them?'

'You're a protestant, aren't you?'

'I'm a protestant by birth all right but I was never that damnfool sort of protestant.'

It was the nearest they ever came to acidity.

'I'm glad again because you'll like him. Professionally he services Lucia's soul but he's a great deal more than a mere *parocco*. And he leaves mine strictly alone, which is civilized. He's a catholic of course, so he can't be a Calvinist, but I suspect he's a raving Jansenist privately. Since I'm obviously damned he respects my damnation.'

'A gentleman's approach.'

'He is that.'

There was a noise from the front door as it opened and Lucia came in with the smiling priest. He shook hands with her husband and came over to Russell. 'Father Gabriel,' Mrs Mortimer said. 'This is the Colonel Russell we spoke of.'

'I have always wanted to meet you.'

'That's kind.'

They made small talk over glasses of sherry and Russell looked hard at the priest without seeming to. He wore a clerical collar, Roman style, but an ordinary suit which was carefully kept. He was of Russell's age or a year or two less and his English was very fluent indeed, innocent of the local accent. Clearly he'd been to school in England and Russell could make a guess at which school. He was a protestant Anglo-Irishman and therefore good at judging priests. A Jesuit — he'd bet a monkey. He was a little surprised but didn't show it, for he'd heard that the late Prime Minister loathed them. Well, he wouldn't have been the first ruler to do so.

They went into the dining-room and the priest said a grace before sitting down. Mortimer had said he was talkative but with food on his plate he attacked that first. Considering she'd lost her shopping the cook had produced a minor miracle. Russell had expected cold luncheon but there was sole and then a *coq-au-vin*. The priest emitted the faintest burp, not so loud he was obliged to apologize, then leant back in his chair with his glass half empty. Instantly the manservant filled it.

'One thing about our late Prime Minister. He improved our wine out of all recognition.'

'So I have noticed,' Russell said.

'Have you noticed anything else?'

'Not a lot. But Robert has told me the local set-up.' There was some emphasis on the adjective 'local' and the priest, who'd been trained to do so, noticed it.

'Then I'm here to talk of the international.' For a moment he was silent, thinking; he was putting his thoughts in logical order; he'd been a teacher in a seminary and therefore better than good at exegesis. He said at length:

'So you know local form. *Quod principi placuit legis habet vigorem.*' He translated for Mrs Mortimer's benefit. 'What pleases the ruler the law will support.' That comes from a Royal Commission, you know, and was written in eighteen hundred and twelve. So we've always been much as you see us today. There are people who think the Fox revolutionary, but he isn't that, he's almost feudal. The difference is he's a *native* lord. We're not a foreign fief any more and for that we put up with a good deal of nonsense.'

'Nonsense?'

'Oh yes, there's a good deal of nonsense. You've heard of Building a Bridge between East and West?' The capitals came across in mockery. 'The Fox inherited that but he isn't stupid; he knows that he hasn't a hope of bringing it off. We haven't the bricks to start building anything.'

'But surely with Arab aid —'

'I concede it. With Arab aid we can do a good deal, though ultimately we shall have to pay for it, but it doesn't alter the facts of geography. All *realpolitik* has its roots in geography.' Father Gabriel's glass was empty again and he waited while the manservant filled it; he took a generous mouthful and then went on, 'It's fashionable in certain circles to assert that all bases are out of date. I venture to dissent rather strongly. Situated where we are we'd still be of something more than value to whoever managed to get here first. To that extent the theory's mistaken, but it wouldn't end at theory. It couldn't. If the West got here first as you very well might — ' Russell noticed 'you' but didn't comment — 'the East wouldn't leave you in peaceful possession. It might try a counter-invasion — I doubt it. There'll not be a second Great Siege of this Island. The East would simply take us out, and soft as you are in the West today if it went the other way round you'd do the same. A nuke would come down and that would be that. There wouldn't be any base. Nor an Island.'

'You should have been a soldier, sir.'

'To tell you the truth I did once think of it.' He was too courteous to explain his choice. He had decided most military men were bores.

Charles Russell reflected before asking a question. 'You think the Fox is scared of that?'

'Not more than any sensible man. It's something that could happen tomorrow and none of us has the least control of it. But you're right if you're hinting the Fox is scared.'

'Of economic penetration?'

The Jesuit smiled the cool smile of his Order. 'That's already gone far too far to halt. There's something called the House of Friendship and it's a front for the money they're pouring in. The decision to do so was taken jointly, to treat us as part of the Arab world, but joint decisions by the Arab League are about as effective as those in New York. That means that they're completely futile without a Power which is ready to back them actively, and where we're concerned that Power is Saliya. If they chose they could pull out the rug tomorrow. Ship-repairing would go broke in a week and our light industries wouldn't be far behind them. One man in two would be unemployed and we couldn't just ship them off to Australia. That boom is over. They found us out.'

'And the Fox is frightened of that?'

'Of course. But he's extremely good at walking a tight-rope.'

'Then what's his *real* fear?'

'Of straight invasion.'

Charles Russell began to protest gently. 'Militarily I doubt if it's on. Saliya has an army of sorts but it's notoriously ill-trained and ill-led. And there's two hundred miles of sea between you. They'd need landing craft and logistic support and from what I hear that's quite beyond them.'

'Have you also heard that they're training paratroops?'

'I hadn't but it makes little difference. One lesson we learnt from the Second World War was that paratroops alone can do little. They need airborne guns and light armour to back them. The Russians have eight airborne *Divisions* but I'm certain enough that Saliya has none.'

'Suppose they dropped and captured the port. How long do you think they could hold it?'

'How good is your local Defence Force?'

'Terrible.'

'Then I give them three days.'

'In three days they could easily bring in ships.'

'In three days they could also be out on their ears.'

'Who would put them out? Would you British come back?'

Charles Russell was a tactful man. 'Our departure,' he said, 'was a trifle undignified.'

Father Gabriel laughed. 'Then NATO?'

'Doubtful. The Sixth Fleet judges its risks realistically. It would like this Island back all right, but it wouldn't risk firing on Arab soldiers just for space to put its anchors down. Its real base is Norfolk, State of Virginia.'

'The United Nations?'

'Don't make me laugh.'

'I wasn't intending to make you laugh.'

Russell thought again before he spoke. 'You're chipping away at my confidence, Father.' He seldom addressed a priest as 'father' but then he had very few dealings with priests.

Father Gabriel smiled his professional smile.

'It's one of the first techniques we learn. But I don't mean to chip too far or too deeply. There'll be no invasion tomorrow morning. But I'm suggesting you leave your high horses behind you.' It was spoken without the least offence, one intelligent man mildly chiding another.

'I wasn't a mounted officer.'

'That I know. But the eastern Med isn't easy to read and Saliya's ruler has foolish amibitions.'

'Which brings an invasion nearer?'

'By no means. Wars aren't started by human frailties but by events which are historically necessary. The Marxist word is ineluctable.'

'Is that sound doctrine?'

'No, it's a heresy. But as you've probably guessed I'm not a Dominican.'

Mrs Mortimer hadn't spoken a word, but now she looked at the clock and rose. They all rose with her and went to the door. At it the priest said softly to Russell:

'Don't stay here too long, my agreeable friend.'

'Aren't you contradicting yourself?'

'Yes, in a sense, but a priest is allowed to. I told you there'd be no invasion tomorrow but if they find an excuse I think they'll take action.'

'What sort of excuse?'

'But that's *their* secret.'

Concerta was sitting quietly at home but still dressed to leave her flat again. She had shut up her shop but would have to revisit it for she was expecting a consignment at nine. The secret of her surprising success in a country which kept its women subservient was that she never bought anything less than the best, and the best could often come from a distance, some herd still in reasonably competent hands. Those hands could be Arab and so unpredictable. She might very well have to wait till midnight but just once in twenty times they were punctual. In which case they'd take offence at your absence; they wouldn't wait for you or ring your flat; they'd simply go off in a huff, meat and all. She couldn't afford to have that happen so she collected a book and cigarettes, prepared to sit it out till they came.

The shop was an easy walk and she went on foot. Astonishingly she found it padlocked and a policeman was lolling against the door. 'You can't go in,' he said unnecessarily.

She thought it over: this might be police blackmail. Such things had happened before and would happen again.

'You feel I need protection?' she asked. If that were it the Crown would be furious.

'I don't feel you need anything, Miss. I'm acting under the highest order.'

'Whose orders, may I ask?'

'The Crown's.'

At first she didn't believe what she'd heard, then sat down on a crate a little shakily. She lit one of her cigarettes and thought carefully. If this wasn't a trick, which it didn't now look like, the man was throwing her out like a whore. She was more than a little Saliyan by now : they had even made love in Maghrebi Arabic. Suddenly she was wholly an Islander.

'I'd like to go in for a moment, please.'

'You can't do that.'

She produced her purse. 'I only want a souvenir. You can come with me and no one will know.'

The policeman eyed her purse. 'How much?' She named a figure, he promptly doubled it. They haggled for a while, then struck.

He took off the padlock and Concerta went in, the policeman behind her watching closely. She went to the butchery counter and looked at it. Behind it were hanging her tools in a row. She was a craftswoman and they were spotlessly clean. She took down a heavy cleaver, balancing it. There was a bone on the counter and she suddenly struck at it. Once did it. There were now two bones.

She put the cleaver in her bag and went out. The policeman turned out the light and replaced the padlock. Unexpectedly he said:

'I'm sorry.'

'It isn't your fault. You have your orders.'

She went back to her flat and found her passport. She had a little money and took that too. It wouldn't be worth a lot on the Island but she could think of no good reason to leave it. Anyway she would need an air ticket. Everything else she left without a qualm. This life was over. Regrets were behind her.

She took out her little car and got in. Her bag was on the seat beside her. Then she drove to the Crown's surburban villa.

A sentry was on the door as usual but he knew her and stood aside at once. He didn't salute but was very polite.

'He's upstairs in bed.'

'That's where I'd expected to find him.'

The sentry grinned and waved her on.

She had put on rubber-soled shoes and moved quietly. . . . Up the staircase and the first to the left. She was moving in the dark for she knew the way. At his door she turned the handle carefully. She had noticed that it sometimes squeaked. She inched the door open but this time noiselessly.

In the room there was a faint light from a street lamp. The Crown was lying in bed on his back, his torso bare.

She stared at his face with a cool detachment. Like many Maghrebis he looked somehow indeterminate. He hadn't an Arab's commanding features and equally he wasn't negroid. Bastards, she thought — they're all of them bastards.

She crept closer to the bed on tiptoe for his face was not her chosen target. She balanced the cleaver and then struck once. She hesitated but then pulled the sheet up. It seemed improper to leave him bare like that.

She went down the stairs again, this time openly. The sentry looked surprised so she spoke to him.

'He looked terribly tired so I didn't wake him.'

The sentry thought that this was considerate. He permitted a smile. 'Another time?'

'Perhaps,' she said but she knew there would not be.

'If you didn't wake him nor will I.'

'That's right. Just let him sleep it out.'

'Good night to you, Miss.'

'Good night to you, Corporal.'

She climbed into her car and drove to the airport. She knew there was a flight at midnight.

She was a craftswoman and respected her tools. She'd kept one of them still and she'd keep it for ever.

On the aircraft, in the loo, she washed it.

Charles Russell was woken at two by an argument. He wasn't one of nature's eavesdroppers but his room was next to Robert Mortimer's and with the windows open and voices raised he couldn't help hearing the altercation. For that was what it was, a domestic row.

Robert was almost shouting. 'She did *what*?'

'I told you. She killed him.'

'How did she kill him?'

'She chopped his head off.'

There was an incredulous silence, a burst of Islander. Robert was clearly asking questions and Russell, since hear he must, was annoyed. So somebody, a woman at that, had cut off somebody's head, a man's. Interesting in itself — most unusual. More interesting to know the details but he didn't know a word of Islander.

But they had dropped back into English again. Robert was asking:

'How do you know?'

'Concerta told me herself. She's down at the airport.'

. . . Concerta. That was Robert's wife's sister.

'*Is* she?'Robert made it sound menacing. An oath would have been forgiven easily but Mortimer detested swearing.

'I can't understand why you're so upset. Put your clothes on, dear, and go and fetch her.'

'But she's killed a man.'

'No doubt with good reason.' It was the patient voice of a wife of long standing.

'Anyway, we can't have her here.'

'Why ever not?'

Robert had almost lost his temper. 'Woman, I beg you to think. Just think. They'll apply for extradition tomorrow.'

'No dear, it's you who must do the thinking. The Crown of the Faithful killed by his mistress? His head cut off like a chicken's? No.'

. . . So that's whom she's done, the Crown of the Faithful. The Crown and the head that wore it too.

Mrs Mortimer was going on placidly. 'They'll hush the whole thing up. They must.'

'They'll find out that she's gone to earth with us. They've a man here, a Greek, and they pay him well.'

'I would guess that they know what you do already.'

'That's probably true.' Another silence. 'But I still don't like it.'

'Nor do I.' Lucia produced her trump, an ace. 'But she's your sister-in-law,' she said. 'She's family.' It was a blow below the belt, a woman's.

Robert, said something in outraged Islander. Lucia said simply: 'Now get up and fetch her.'

There was no more talk but the sounds of dressing. Presently a door slammed angrily. A minute later he heard a car start.

Charles Russell went to sleep again. It was none of his business, he'd heard what he shouldn't. But he was looking forward to breakfast next morning. She sounded quite a woman, Concerta.

4

Charles Russell was disappointed next morning when Concerta didn't appear at breakfast. Mrs Mortimer, pouring coffee, said steadily:

'I'm sorry if the car woke you last night. We've had an unexpected visitor and Robert had to go to the airport. It's my sister Concerta who stayed on in Saliya. She's not been well and the doctors aren't good there, so she's decided to come to us for a time. A doctor is with her now as it happens, and I expect he'll keep her quiet for a bit.'

Charles Russell nodded: so far this was true. He had seen a strange car on his way to breakfast, and a woman who'd killed a man like a chicken could be forgiven if she needed a sedative. Naturally it wasn't all the truth, but the rest of it Russell had overheard. He didn't like overhearing things and when he did he had a time-proven maxim; he tried to expunge what he'd heard completely and as often as not he succeeded in doing so.

'I hope she gets well soon.'

'So do I.'

Robert Mortimer rose with a brief apology. 'I've got to go down to the office this morning and Lucia will be nursing her sister. I hope the morning won't drag on your hands.'

'There are things I'd like to see again. I'll go for a walk and take some in.'

He took his hat and a stick but he didn't walk far. Instead

he sat down in the sun to think, for he would have confessed that he was more than curious. This was really a very unusual *ménage*, though there'd been nothing until the affair last night which couldn't be explained away if explaining away was what you wanted. Charles Russell did not but he mistrusted coincidence. Starting at the beginning, then, Mortimer was living in considerable style, much greater than Russell had ever imagined. Explanation of that? He had come into money. Alternatively he had mentioned a business, but he didn't behave like a business man. He had a room in the house with a desk and a telephone, but none of the apparatus of business, no filing cabinets, no daily secretary. And if his main place of business was somewhere else this was the first morning he'd gone there.

And he stood exceptionally well with officialdom. That interview at Immigration had been teetering on the brink of unpleasantness till a mention of Robert Mortimer's name had led to something quite close to welcome. Was Robert some sort of official himself? Charles Russell shook his head at once. If he were he was remarkably well paid, far too well for a man who could go to his office apparently once in three days at most. And there was something else against that theory. In this queer little faintly sinister stateling no official would sit while a priest talked critically, far less invite him to luncheon to do so. Moreover Mortimer too had talked — of houses of political enemies which inexplicably went up in smoke, of yachts which disappeared at sea. In this sort of not-quite-police-state-nor-a-free-one rumour was in the air men breathed, but Mortimer wasn't a man to pass rumours. Russell believed he'd been passing a message, one he preferred not to pass expressly. What message? Russell didn't know that yet but he wouldn't go seeking the key: it would come to him. A lifetime's experience told him that and meanwhile the sun was warm and his muscles loosening.

He had intended to take a trip round the harbour and he looked at his map for the way to the jetties from which the tourist launches started. It seemed about two miles at the most, a pleasant stroll before the sun gathered bite. He folded his map and set off briskly.

It was a straightforward route by a road round the creek but Russell had seen an enchanting side street, had been tempted and at once had fallen. The street went slightly uphill but not tiringly and as he walked the ambience changed dramatically. There were the unmistakable sounds and smells of Arab life, the feeling of indifference to the standards of European man. Also there were several women and these women weren't Arab women; they were whores.

Russell went into a bar and bought a beer. The barkeeper was an Islander and he looked at Russell a little curiously. Presently he came across to his table.

'Excuse me, sir. Do you know where you are?'

'I don't know the name of the area — no.'

'It is Xalah and it's the Saliyan quarter.'

'That I had rather gathered.'

'Alas. We've lived here for several generations and resent that it's been taken over. There were fine houses once.'

'There seem to be still.'

'But do not go inside one, sir. Wherever an Arab goes he brings filth.'

It was an exaggeration and a bitter one but Russell could understand and sympathize. He bought the barman his morning brandy and as it warmed him he began to talk freely.

'Are you carrying much money, sir?'

'No, not a lot.'

'That's just as well. But keep it in an inside pocket.' He got up and brought beer and another brandy. 'May I ask why you came here? It's not for tourists.'

'I was walking along the road by the sea and I thought it looked a nice street.'

'It was. Now it's something between a slum and a whorehouse. Did you see many women?'

'Several women.'

'That's what they come here for — the Saliyans, I mean. The rich ones who work in the House of Friendship are settled here and live in villas but the houses round this part are now mostly flats. The Saliyans rent them for a week or a fortnight and in that time they booze like pigs and lech. The former their ruler officially frowns on and the latter, though it isn't illegal, isn't something to risk in Saliya too often. On top of that they behave like animals, swaggering about and fighting. Naturally we resent it furiously.'

'Don't the police interfere?'

'The police do not dare. This traffic brings in a lot of money and on top of that the Saliyans half own us. Anything which looked like prejudice would bring instant diplomatic protest and that's the last thing our Chief Executive wants.'

'Can you do nothing yourselves?'

'We try. We have unofficial vigilantes but they don't do much more than bash and run. Those Saliyans have knives and sometimes guns. In any case we can't risk real trouble. There've been a couple of minor clashes, quite small ones, but anything like a real riot and we've had it. We'd be on the other island next day.'

Charles Russell understood him perfectly. There was another and very much smaller island, a prison with a grim reputation. Men went there and not always came back.

But the barkeeper was talking again. 'None of which helps us to hate them less. One day there's going to be serious trouble. It won't be nice for the people of Xalah and it's going to put our master on the spot.' He seemed to be going to say more but didn't. 'May I ask where you were going, sir?'

'I was intending to take a trip round the harbour.'

'You can just about make the last departure. I'll ring for a taxi but don't speak of what I have.'

The guides were still standing beside their launches, touting for custom from coaches and taxis. Russell chose not the largest launch but the one which carried a woman guide. A man mouthing the same rigmarole daily was quick to acquire a manner of boredom but a woman seemed to be more resistant. He paid his fare and chose a seat.

The beer had made him a little drowsy for it wasn't his normal morning drink but the woman's spiel kept him wide awake. It was slick but also well-informed. She pointed out the splendid old buildings with a warm respect and even love; she had a pleasantly astringent word for later accretions less than admirable. She spoke of the Siege but not too much. It was an incident in the Island's long history and it mightn't have occurred at all if the Order hadn't broken its word. She had a pleasant sense of irony too. When they came to the broken lighthouse causeway she explained about the Italian navy. It had made a sensational raid by night, puffing it up as a great naval victory. But she'd added straight-faced and in just the same tone that that had been thirty years ago. Passengers would no doubt observe that the causeway had been left unrepaired. Now the lighthouse-keeper went out in a motor boat.

They went round the point to the major harbour and Charles Russell looked around him curiously. It had changed since he had seen it last. Then it had been crowded with warships, the ships of every Allied Power, the aircraft carrier they'd never quite sunk. Now it was crowded still but differently, a Russian cruise liner, assorted merchantmen, and the Saliyan packet half-way to Marseilles, slick in the bright new paint which oil bought for her. The docks were apparently thriving too, and again the guide produced a shrewd comment. They still paid their way though they were now a co-operative. Charles Russell began to like her greatly.

Just before they turned for home he saw something which made him sit up sharply. It was a survey ship, very smart and tight, her decks crowded with electronic equipment. At her stern she flew the flag of the Netherlands and in less conspicuous places two others, the Island's one and

Saliya's the other. Charles Russell interrupted seldom but now he asked sharply:

'What ship is that?'

He thought that for a moment she hesitated. 'She's looking for oil.'

'Has she found it yet?'

'I don't know that — I'm a private citizen.' Another hesitation, then: 'But if they do we'll be really free at last. Not *talking* free, not playing it big, but able to choose our own way and to pay for it.'

Russell nodded his thanks and returned to silence. He'd confirmed what the barman had told him earlier. Not everybody on this very strange Island — not everybody loved Saliyans.

As he left the launch he tipped the guide generously. He thought she'd been worth every penny he gave her.

The sun and the sea had made him thirsty and he saw that he had time for a drink. He went into a bar and sat down, and another man rose from his table and joined him.

'Hullo, old boy.'

'I wish you good morning.'

Russell disliked being called 'old boy', particularly by Sir Perry Mare. He had met him more than once and loathed him. He was a journalist of a peculiar kind, not the sort you would expect to find knighted. Knighted journalists had their own strong odour — weighty articles in the Sunday papers, thoughtful profiles of very eminent people. But Sir Perry had never written either. He was of what Russell called the Mindless Left. . . . If it was old, well-rooted, reputable, you attacked it as a matter of course, made a scandal if you could possibly raise one. And on one of these forays Perry Mare had struck gold. The days of Parnell were long since vanished, no government collapsed next morning because a Minister had been less than continent. But a girl of thirteen, which was statutory rape, the rapist very senior indeed. . . .

Mare had beavered away till he had it on ice, then he'd sold the story but not to his newspaper. Like many men of the far, far Left at heart he was a screaming snob and his first price had been a demand for a peerage. That had been a little too steep even for a man who'd been frightened, but in the end Perry Mare had got his knighthood. There'd been some very odd Honours in recent years but Russell thought Mare's the oddest easily.

Now he had sat down uninvited. 'What are you drinking?'

'I have one, thank you.'

Mare ordered neat whisky and drank it greedily, then he told the waiter to bring the bottle. Charles Russell didn't like Sir Perry and soaks he detested by instinct and training. Sir Perry asked rudely:

'What are you doing here?'

'I'm having a little holiday.'

'And I'm supposed to believe you?'

'Why not?' The technique with boors was to keep your temper but Russell was having some trouble in doing so. He looked at his watch but Sir Perry ignored it.

'So you're here on holiday?'

'Yes, I said so.'

'Staying with whom you are? I've discovered that.'

'Why shouldn't I stay with a friend?'

'Some friend. Do you know what he does?'

'Unlike yourself I'm not overly curious.'

The snub went over Sir Perry's head. He had drunk perhaps a third of his bottle and though far from drunk he had taken drink. He said suddenly:

'There's a story on this Island — a big one.'

'I imagine so or you wouldn't be here.'

Sir Perry exploded noisily. 'It was bad enough under that old Prime Minister. Now the place is a fascist camp.'

It was a word which annoyed Charles Russell intensely. Once it had possessed a meaning, a precise political definition. He could think of two states which had once been fascist and Hitler's Third Reich had not been one of them. Now it was debased to abuse, the snide currency of the Perry Mares.

'You think it's as bad as that?'

'I tell you it's going up in flames.'

'Somebody is going to bomb it?'

'Don't play with me, Russell — I don't like that.'

'Guilty,' Charles Russell told him mildly.

'The whole Island is on a knife edge and wobbling. I've come here to get the story.'

'So you said.'

'What do want to cut me in? I'm getting quite near but I don't have the key yet.'

'If I had a story I wouldn't peddle it.'

'Bollocks,' Sir Perry Mare said promptly.

Charles Russell half rose but sat down again quickly. 'But one thought does occur.'

'Please tell me.' He had changed in an instant from bully to beggar.

'If this Island is really the pit of reaction which I gather you've decided it is shouldn't you move with a certain caution?'

'What can they do to me?'

'That I don't know.'

'I'm a reputable journalist.'

'Yes? Indeed?'

'I don't like your manner.'

'I think I can bear it.'

Mare's voice changed yet again, to sly. 'I saw you come off a trip round the harbour. No doubt you noticed that Dutch survey ship. What do you suppose she was doing there?'

'Looking for oil.'

'Of course. But where?'

'In the sea, I imagine.'

'Quite so. But whose sea? There've been quarrels about sea oil before now. Once there was very nearly a war.'

'Is that the story you're grubbing about for?'

'One aspect of it. Yes indeed. The rest I intend to get too.'

'Not from me.'

Sir Perry sneered; it didn't suit him. 'You're working for the Fox. I know it.'

This time Charles Russell rose for good. 'Sir Perry Mare,' he said, 'you're a fool.'

In the heat of the day Russell took his siesta, coming down to a well-dressed young man in the sitting-room. He was clearly an Arab but not a Maghrebi, and he rose at once as Charles Russell came in.

'I didn't like to disturb your rest. Mrs Mortimer asked me to wait till you woke.'

'That was kind of you both.'

The young man smiled, handing Russell an envelope. On the back was an embassy's arms. Russell knew them.

'May I open this?'

'Of course. Please do.'

My very dear friend [the letter ran]

You must think me very rude indeed that I haven't written before to thank you, but the first few days after any incident are days which have to be handled with care. I did ring twice and both times missed you, then I learnt that you'd gone to the Island on holiday. Frankly, I very much wish you hadn't. I may be an unconventional President [an understatement, Russell thought with a smile] *and my trips abroad may cause embarrassment, but as a Head of State I have certain perquisites and one of them is good Intelligence.*

Charles, if I may so address you, I don't like the smell of that Island at all. I dare say you've rumbled the general background — a man of your experience would — but there's something rather more than general, and you're a man with a reputation which you'd like to escape from but never can. Had you thought of that? Of a misunderstanding? Here's the Head of the Security Executive — I beg your pardon, the ex-Head; no matter — arriving in a notorious wasps' nest. There are men who wouldn't believe for a moment that he'd gone there on an innocent holiday, in which case they would ask themselves: Which side is he on, to which side a danger?

You may think me an impertinent fool but I beg you to leave the Island at once. If you won't do that, as I fear you will not, at the least sign of danger go straight to my embassy. I have given it orders to receive and protect you.

Charles Russell read this twice, then looked up. 'You know the contents of this letter?'

'I do. Naturally it came in cipher. I decoded it myself and typed it.'

'Your President is very thoughtful.'

'My President owes you his life.'

'Hardly that.'

'The important thing is he thinks he does, and he's a man who pays his debts. Either way.'

'Can you send a reply?'

'Of course. Please dictate it.'

The young man produced a pad and pencil and Russell dictated a brief polite answer. The President was more than kind, and yes, he had noticed an air of unease, but he'd been in uneasy countries before and had survived to write this letter of thanks. In any case he was staying with friends, one of his own men as it happened. But he'd bear what the President said in mind and he gratefully remembered his offer.

The young man put his pad away, carefully destroying the undersheet. He shook hands and took his leave with a bow.

Over the first of his evening's whiskies Charles Russell frowned at familiar signals. Robert Mortimer's household was concealing a killer; a barkeeper had been frightened of rioting; a woman on a boat had been delphic; and Sir Perry Mare had been sniffing obscenely. He had even claimed Russell worked for the Fox. Perry Mare was a drunken but knighted hack, the product of his background and age, but the assertion had been made with confidence. There were other and more intelligent men who might conceivably draw the same conclusion.

And now the President had seen fit to warn him, and one thing that man was not was stupid. But warn him of what? That wasn't yet clear. He had come here as an honest visitor and of one aspect he was entirely sure: Robert Mortimer would never have cheated, luring him into some local involvement on the pretext of suggesting a holiday. Involvements, he thought — he didn't want one. No, but they sometimes entrapped him against his will.

There was a risk no doubt, but he'd have to accept it. The alternative was to pack and run, and that would lie on his mind till he died.

He finished the first of his ration reflectively. Another thought had crept in and Charles Russell mistrusted it.

If anything happened he might even enjoy it.

Sir Perry had been on his evening bar crawl. He could take a great deal and he wasn't blind drunk, but nor was he entirely sober. He took a taxi to his hotel and dismissed it, tipping a little less than was normal. He wouldn't have tipped at all but for fear. In his hotel the night clerk stopped him politely.

'There's a gentleman to see you, sir.'

Sir Perry said: 'Where?' and looked round the hall. He could see nobody he knew or wished to.

'I sent him up to your room, sir?'

'You did *what*?'

'He's an official. I thought it wiser — discreeter.'

'I'll have your liver,' Sir Perry said.

The night clerk didn't move a muscle. He was accustomed to discourteous foreigners and was generously paid to suffer their arrogance, but he had his own means to settle a private score. Once Sir Perry was safely inside the lift he telephoned to Accounts. Someone laughed.

In Perry Mare's room a man rose to meet him. 'I have come from Immigration,' he said.

Sir Perry had taken a good deal of drink but now he began to sober quickly. He'd told Russell he'd come quite close to a story, and if that story were what he guessed it would make an immediate, screaming headline. 'Immigration', he thought — they were going to frame him. This had happened to him twice before and he knew the drill or thought he did.

'My passport is in perfect order.' He went to a drawer and took it out, but the official waved it aside indifferently.

'Your passport is indeed in order. Unfortunately your entry is not.'

Mare looked at the passport. 'It says a month.'

'Also "Declared Purpose: Tourist." '

'But I haven't been working,' Sir Perry said. But he said it more than a little defensively, for a local paper had asked for a piece and he'd done them an innocent puff for the Island. They'd offered an honorarium, twenty-five pounds in Island money, which Sir Perry had thought distinctly mean. He had realized that he shouldn't take it but he'd been greedy and in the end had accepted. Twenty-five pounds was several bottles of whisky.

'We have a statement that you've accepted money in the exercise of your normal profession.'

'Twenty-five pounds — a mere politeness. It's the custom of my profession, you know.'

'It is also a breach of the terms of your entry.' The official's manner stiffened suddenly. 'I believe you hold an open ticket.'

Sir Perry nodded.

'That is fortunate — it avoids arresting you. There's a flight at two o'clock this morning and naturally we have reserved a seat for you.'

The drink was dying fast in Sir Perry but not his established, instinctive habits. Immediately he began to bluster.

'You can't do this to me.'

'I have orders.'

'I can make it very awkward for you. I'm pretty well known where I come from.'

'No doubt. Where you come from, however, is not this Island.' The official looked at his watch. 'We are late. I'll accompany you to the airport and see you through. Now I must ask you to pack. Ten minutes.'

In the foyer Sir Perry asked for his bill, staring at it in total amazement. It was fifty pounds more than he had expected and included two dozen of local red wine.

'But I never drink wine,' he said, 'or not yours.'

The night clerk was calm; he had done this before. 'Would you like to see the chits, sir?'

'Certainly.'

The night clerk picked the telephone up and a man appeared with a biggish bundle. Mostly they were from one of the bars but there were others which had come from the restaurant. Mare looked at several of these and frowned.

'But this isn't my signature.'

'Sir, it must be.'

'I can only tell you again that it isn't.'

The night clerk's politeness changed at once. Previously he'd been bored but courteous; now he was suddenly cold and formidable. 'That's an extremely serious accusation. The manager is of course in bed but I have standing instructions to ring him at once in any matter which could involve the Courts. I expect he will bring our lawyer with him.'

The Immigration man had been standing silently; now he looked at his watch again and spoke.

'If we don't catch that plane I must make other arrangements. Shortly, I must call the police.'

Sir Perry cursed but he paid the bill.

At the airport they sat down and waited. The official chain-smoked and Mare drank from his flask. His passport had been taken away and presently a man handed it back. His entry stamp had been cancelled flamboyantly. Two parallel red lines had been ruled through it and underneath was stamped in bold capitals:

TERMINATED DUE TO BREACH OF CONDITIONS

... Even the Israelis didn't do that to me.

When the flight was called the official went with him but he didn't carry Sir Perry's cabin bag. He saw him up the steps to the aircraft, and half-way up Sir Perry turned. He couldn't resist a parting shot but it wasn't in any sense a good one. 'I'll get you for this,' he shouted. 'Just wait.'

The official didn't even shrug. He watched Mare as he disappeared inside, then turned on his heel and walked away. Against all the rules he was still smoking strongly.

In the hotel the night clerk had picked up the phone again. 'The usual terms?' he asked. 'Fifty-fifty?'

Again the first answer was simply a laugh. Then the official said amiably: 'That's okay.'

5

The man whom Mahmud had called that damned Greek was a Greek in fact and very probably damned, at least in the eyes of those who knew him. He was a Levantine and mainland Greeks despised him, suspecting he had all their vices but less than a proper share of their gifts. In this they were something less than fair: he was clever, observant and instinctively devious. He was the Crown of the Faithful's ear on the Island for he hadn't been trained as an active agent. In any case the House of Friendship had been salted with every kind of operator. But as a listening post his peculiar talents were well employed and his masters knew it. He picked up every snippet of rumour, of gossip even when rumour failed, and this he passed back as he heard it, unedited. He wasn't required to evaluate for the very good reason he wasn't trusted to.

For these services he was handsomely paid. He drew a regular retaining fee but for the rest he was paid by results. Unpredictably. For instance, that last piece he'd sent them, that the sister of the President's mistress had a husband who was the Fox's agent — he had expected a generous recognition but what he had received had been minimal. It was the more puzzling since he knew his paymasters. He was a Greek with the logical mind of his race and the fact that Concerta's sister, Lucia, had a husband in the Fox's service proved nothing about Concerta herself. He wouldn't even have made a bet on it, but then he was a Greek, not an Arab.

Arabs had their own illogic imposed on them by ancestral habit. Intrigue and the double cross were in their blood. Feed them something which looked vaguely suspicious and the last thing they would do would be check it. Hard evidence didn't mean a thing: they'd go flaming away in some furious action.

And nothing of the sort had happened. His news had been received quite calmly and they'd sent him what they usually sent him for some titbit about the Fox's private life.

He was more than puzzled, he felt actively injured. Moreover he needed more money and urgently.

It came to his quick mind in a flash. Colonel Charles Russell, ex-Head of the British Security Executive, was staying in Robert Mortimer's house. Again that wasn't evidence of anything more than an innocent meeting, since Mortimer had once worked for Russell, and what more natural than a friendly visit? But an Arab wouldn't see it like that; he'd think of Charles Russell's reputation. He'd take the single fact which was known and established, that Robert Mortimer worked for the Island's Fox, and round it he'd weave a great web of suspicion — that Russell had come with some sinister purpose, and obviously he wouldn't have done so unless the Fox had badly needed his help. And why would the Fox need Russell's help? Only if he had some counter plan, and that must be nipped in the bud immediately.

Whereupon any Arab would over-react. Almost certainly he'd do something violent, but that wasn't a matter for a good Attic conscience.

The Greek sent his message and sat back, confident. This one would bring him a rich reward. He even paid a bill before he need.

It arrived as the three Young Lions were meeting, Mahmud, the professional soldier, Suleiman, the intellectual, and Sayyid who ran the state's finances, the oil which supported the house of cards. They met twice a week and had need to do so, for each kept a wary eye on the others.

There were Ministers, without power collectively, but these were little more than servants. They accepted the Crown's orders dumbly and when they were not too outrageous obeyed them. In that process they had greatly enriched themselves, but if anything like real power existed outside the hands of the Crown himself it lay in the hands of these three young men, all three ambitious and Mahmud dedicated. They alone held the secret ear of their ruler. That was worth more than official titles.

Suleiman, who ran Intelligence, had opened the message and frozen at once. The other two privately didn't much like him. He had an academic background to start with, and though undoubtedly clever could also be patronizing, giving himself the airs and graces which he believed his education justified. But he ran the Crown's Intelligence well.

'Bad news?' Sayyid asked.

'It's very bad.' He passed round the decoded message, The others took time to think, then Mahmud spoke.

'This will have to go to the Crown at once.'

Sayyid merely nodded and waited. Of the three he alone was thinking lucidly.

Suleiman said: 'Let's toss.'

'By no means.' They had spoken together, a single voice. Mahmud had been caught once before and Sayyid never tossed on principle. 'This is Intelligence — your Department.'

Suleiman didn't like this and said so. The Crown would be in bed with his mistress and had been known to take to violence when disturbed. But it was clear the other two were adamant. Finally he agreed. 'Very well. But you'll wait for me here to hear how he takes it.'

The other men looked at each other unhappily. It was two in the morning and all were sleepless, but in their different ways all had one thing in common. None would shirk what he saw as a necessary duty.

Major Mahmud was the first to speak. 'I've a car outside

and a driver. Take them.'

The other two settled to nap on their chairs and Suleiman drove away uneasily. The sentry was still at the Crown's front door and as Suleiman dismounted said:

'Perhaps you'd better not wake him, sir.'

'What do you mean?' Suleiman thought this impertinent.

'The lady was here a little earlier but she left when she found him fast asleep. She asked me to let him rest if I could.'

'I'm not his mistress and this is state business.' Suleiman had the highbrow's arrogance.

The sentry didn't like it but stepped aside.

Suleiman opened the door and turned on the hall light. He went up the stairs and then left to the bedroom. The light from outside had gone and he flicked the switch.

For the second time that evening he froze. The first time he had frozen in shock but now he froze in simple horror. The sheet had fallen away from the head and Suleiman collapsed in a chair. Understandably he vomited violently.

When the spasms were over he made himself look. The neck might be severed or again it might not. That wasn't important: the rest had been final. A swordsman couldn't have done it more thoroughly.

He went back to his chair and a cigarette. It calmed him but not very much; he was shuddering. When he felt he could walk without collapsing he turned off the bedroom light and tackled the stairs. He went very carefully, holding the banister. At the front door the patient sentry said:

'You weren't very long, sir.'

'I didn't need to be.'

He climbed into Major Mahmud's car.

Thank God that the other two were waiting. He couldn't have handled this alone.

Suleiman had blurted the news out in horror, for a moment in something very near panic. He himself, still in shock, had collapsed in a chair, but Mahmud was striding the room in a fury, demanding an immediate vengeance. Their collective honour had been rolled in the gutter, they must all three go to the woman's house. . . .

Sayyid had partly recovered first, going to the telephone, returning to the others grimly. 'A woman caught the midnight flight. She had nothing but a handbag — no luggage. She bought a single ticket. She's gone.'

Mahmud began to talk wildly of following but Sayyid let him talk on without answering. Of the three he was the toughest mentally, less emotionally involved than Mahmud, less prone to the intellectual's doubts and fears. He had seen the essential at once and grasped it. Their immediate problem was not the Crown's death but the manner in which he had met his end. The Crown of the Faithful cut down by his mistress, an unbelieving, a foreign mistress at that. . . . Such a story could tear the frail state to pieces.

Mahmud was still in a haze of fury and Sayyid said to him sharply: 'Sit down.'

Mahmud sat. Imperceptibly Sayyid was taking charge and Mahmud recognized the cool voice of authority.

....Had Mahmud two men he could really trust? One of them ought to be a doctor.

Yes, he had his sergeant-major, a kinsman of his he could wholly rely on, and there was a doctor at the training camp whom Mahmud had once saved from a scandal.

And was there perhaps a stand-by coffin?

Yes, there was a coffin.

Good. Then all three were to go to the Crown's house immediately. Put the body in the coffin and seal it. The doctor must choose the cause of death but heart failure from overwork would probably best appeal to the people. Clean the room up — I would guess there'd be vomit — and anything bloodstained to go in the coffin. If you have to cut up the mattress do so.

Mahmud had begun to think too. 'And the sentry?' he asked.

'I can see no problem. You tell him the truth or rather part of it. When Suleiman called earlier he found that the Crown was dead. That is true. In any event of such obvious import he would hurry away to consult his colleagues, not stand gossiping with a simple soldier.'

Mahmud thought this over carefully. 'There's a chance,' he said at the end.

'Then take it. Go to that phone and give the orders.'

When Mahmud returned the first tension had eased. With God's blessing they were over one hurdle but another was ahead more formidable. Suleiman had come out of his shock and it was he who finally asked:

'What now?'

The others understood him perfectly: he was talking of the political future. They'd been the three most powerful men in the country but they'd been so by crowding the late Crown's ear. If they put themselves forward, a sort of triumvirate, few men would even know their names, and no Minister carried the weight to succeed. They were nonentities and had been chosen as such. The Crown had no legitimate son so there couldn't be any question of regency. All three reached the same conclusion together but it was Mahmud who voiced it.

'We must go to the General.'

'It's that or chaos. We'll go to him at eight o'clock. Meanwhile we ought to try to sleep.'

They'd been meeting in Sayyid's modest flat which had only one bedroom and only one bed, and good manners demanded that Sayyid should offer it. Immediately there was an altercation. In most countries outside the Arab world the matter would have been settled pragmatically: Suleiman had suffered the biggest shock so Suleiman had most need of rest. But the fear of losing face was paramount. Mahmud was a serving soldier, so it was unthinkable to take a bed while civilians sat on chairs or lay on the floor. Sayyid was the host and an Arab. In the end they reached the worst solution, taking the bed to pieces and sharing it. Suleiman agreed to the mattress and the others took a pillow each.

But when he saw that the other two were sleeping Sayyid got up and went to the window. He'd been the first of the three to recover his balance for any crisis released his reserves of energy. The argument about the bed had wasted nearly half an hour and the dawn was coming up in majesty. Sayyid had always loved the dawn and he watched it as it spread in splendour.

He was different from the other two, an upper-crust Arab from far to the east with an Islamic title to prove his ancestry. He seldom used it since he wasn't class conscious but he was conscious of the facts of race. The other two spoke Arabic, though with an accent which he found distressing, and privately he thought them provincial. Major Mahmud lived by a soldier's values and these would always command respect, but Suleiman was an intellectual and suspect of being a pouffe at that. Neither of them would last the course.

But Sayyid would because he'd been taught to. The Crown had employed him to run his oil but by cautious steps which the Crown hadn't noticed he'd moved to controlling the state's finances. There was a Minister of Finance as well in whose name all fiscal matters were dealt with but the real strings ran through Sayyid's fingers.

He was well-qualified to handle them expertly. He had brains and a good degree from America, he had worked in a bank and then in oil. He was more than a quarter westernized and in moments of crisis he thought like a westerner.

He was doing so now for this was a crisis. But not quite the crisis the others thought it. He had agreed at once that they must go to the General: at this moment there wasn't a real alternative if the country were not to fall apart. At this moment, but there was also the future. Military rule would be quietly accepted, or if it were not had the means to impose itself, but it was unlikely that it would last forever. The Ministers were men of straw and the three Young

Lions couldn't rule as a *troika*.

No, but if the three became one. . . .

He moved from the window and shaved his lip thoughtfully, trimming his handsome beard with care. The face in the mirror looked back at him silently. He caught himself with a thought he suppressed. It was the face of one of nature's rulers.

They presented themselves at eight o'clock and the General kept them waiting half an hour. Partly this was a matter of protocol since all of them were much his junior and partly because he was eating his breakfast. When he had finished he had them shown in. It had been agreed that Suleiman tell what he'd found and that Mahmud, who'd made them, should recount the arrangements. The General listened stiff-backed and silent, then asked two brief but pertinent questions.

'Major Mahmud, have you checked your orders?'

'I have checked that they've been carried out, sir.'

'Can you trust these two men to hold their tongues? I can think of a guarantee that they do.'

'I can think of another.'

'Yes? What's that?'

'The fear of ridicule — public ridicule. I propose to confine them to camp for a fortnight. After that if they told a story like this one they'd be laughed at and very possibly lynched.'

'You seem to have thought it out.'

'We have tried.'

The General lit his after-breakfast cigar; he sat on in silence and Sayyid watched him. He hadn't met him before but he knew his background. He'd been appointed for his soldierly virtues, he was loyal and would never have led a *coup*, but Sayyid had been watching him closely and had decided that he had more than that. Perhaps he had established an image and even slightly overplayed it — cropped grey hair and a bristling white moustache, the bluff manner and rather noisy laugh. If he wanted to look like a military mastodon he had certainly succeeded brilliantly. But undoubtedly there was more than that. Under the props was a very shrewd brain.

The General had begun to talk again. 'Gentlemen, my sincerest thanks. Also those of the nation. You have done very well. And now we must think of that country's future.'

He didn't think long but acted promptly, summoning his Chief of Staff and dictating. . . . The nation had suffered a grievous wound and for the moment there was no one to heal it. The army guarded the country's honour and wouldn't fail it in a matter of duty. There'd be elections as soon as events allowed them for it wasn't the army's business to rule. Its business was to keep the peace and that it proposed to do unflinchingly.

It was a parody though he didn't know it, a hotchpotch of dozens of such proclamations. He had spoken it in Maghrebi Arabic but Spanish was its natural language, a manifesto from some banana republic.

When the Chief had gone he returned to the others. 'State funeral of course — I'll see to that. And you gentlemen will brief the Press? I would guess that you'd do that better than I should.'

The three men nodded and the General went on. 'Major Mahmud, you are now a Colonel.' He turned to the others, half formal, half friendly. 'You gentlemen I cannot promote but I can confirm you in your official positions.' The 'official' held a faint tinkle of irony but of the three men only Sayyid noticed it.

. . . And I'm taking a very grave risk in doing so. Mahmud is a serving soldier and is subject to a soldier's disciplines, Suleiman runs the Intelligence Service though I've a private one if it came to a crisis, but Sayyid I cannot do without. I know nothing of oil and less of money. He's the cleverest and therefore most dangerous, but without him we'd go bankrupt tomorrow.

But he showed none of this thought as he rose and

dismissed them. 'No doubt we all have urgent business. All I can do is to thank you again.'

When they'd gone he lit another cigar. The deadpan soldier's face had sharpened. He was considering the future dispassionately since he didn't wish to govern for ever; he wanted to retire to his villa where he had some interesting English roses. What were his chances of that? Not good. He could keep control for several years till the three Young Lions were one Young Lion, but later that might mean a struggle with whichever of the three survived. He corrected himself: whichever of two. Mahmud he thought he could hold fairly easily but the other two were politicians, not subject to a soldier's loyalties, and the nature of political life, especially in an Arab country, made it certain they'd fight until one came out paramount. It wouldn't, he was sure, be Suleiman. He shared Sayyid's opinion, the man was a poof, but Sayyid himself would be very dangerous if he acted too fast and emerged too soon. The General would happily go when the time came but he wanted to leave a stable state to whoever stepped into his vacant shoes.

And of that the chances seemed alarmingly small since both Mahmud and Sayyid were the late Crown's disciples. They'd have inherited his preposterous scheme of trying to take over a neighbouring Island. Mahmud was the late Crown's oblate, training special troops for adventure, and though Sayyid would probably think that foolish the General suspected he had a plan of his own.

Either way such an ambition was madness, for they simply hadn't the base to mount it. The military difficulties apart, and to the General these were distressingly obvious, an invasion of another country demanded that your own be secure. The General knew that Saliya was not. The Saliyans were not a warlike people, they were meek and a couple of shots sent them scampering, but what were officially called Our Guests were men of a more lively temperament. There were thousands of them and the number was growing; they were the doctors and accountants and lawyers; they ran the oil and they ran the banks, always under some indigenous figurehead, invariably the Crown's dependant. Moreover they had a standing grievance, the fact that they weren't paid the rate for the job. In practice they were second-class citizens. They didn't have a vote between them, not even in the rigged elections. Not that votes counted for much but power did. How long would they stand for political impotence when without them quotidian business would collapse?

He put the question aside impatiently since the answer was on the lap of the gods. So far there had been nothing serious, a scuffle or two which the police had dealt with, but these Guests were a time-bomb ticking ominously. They weren't organized — the Crown hadn't allowed it — but most of them came from a single country and in a crunch would surely obey his orders. Its orders meant its President's orders and the late Crown had three times tried to kill him. In the name of what was called Arab unity the President had held his hand, but there was no guarantee he would do so for ever and if he changed his mind the weapon was there still.

The General saw the future bleakly. Of one thing he was entirely certain: the Crown had had the wrong priority and now the Young Lions were glad heirs to his error. Instead of plotting some foolish adventure they should be watching for an explosion at home.

The funeral was very grand indeed. Well-dressed men and women wept in the streets. They wept with the others because they'd been ordered to.

6

The Greek's guess had been right as it often was for the three Young Lions were reacting violently. More precisely Colonel Mahmud was; he was a very angry man and looked it. Suleiman was rather less nervy but was going along with the mood of the meeting. Only Sayyid preserved a secret detachment. He could understand the Colonel's anger for of the three he'd been the closest to the Crown; he'd been his friend as well as his political creature and now he was letting his rage blur intelligence. The quarter of Sayyid's mind which was western could recognize the symtoms clearly. He was arguing with defensible logic from a premise which was far from established. . . . All this was some deep plot by the Fox, the first step in which had been killing the Crown.

Sayyid sat and listened silently. It fitted, no doubt, but not conclusively. The woman had left her car at the airport, buying a single ticket for cash. That didn't look like the planned escape which an agent would have demanded on principle. And she hadn't used an agent's weapon, she had used the tools of her trade in a fury. Sayyid didn't entirely blame her for he thought that the Crown had behaved rather shabbily. Shutting her shop up like that — most insensitive. And he'd been wrong in supposing she'd go straight to her bank. The Crown had thought like that — every man has his price — but he didn't seem very clever with women. Especially with an Islander, who were notoriously hot-blooded and vengeful. So she'd gone back to her sister, another Islander.

A point which Colonel Mahmud was flogging. She'd gone back to her sister who was married to Mortimer, and they'd known for some time that he worked for the Fox. Now that damned Greek was telling them worse: Russell had arrived to join Mortimer. The Fox must have hired him to help in the counter-plot.

Sayyid didn't think this followed. To start with to talk of counter-plots one must be able at least to guess at their nature, and Sayyid himself could make no such guess. The Fox must know the late Crown's intention since it was common chatter where men talked politics, but what plan would help him to counter it wasn't clear. Moreover if there were such a plan, how could Charles Russell help to achieve it? He hadn't an organization behind him, and though he still had influential friends the Fox would have those too and better placed.

But Mahmud was going on remorselessly. He had moved from plots and counter-plots to the matter of simple, naked revenge. It was intolerable to the nation's honour that the murderess of the Crown of the Faithful should be left to enjoy her life in peace.

Sayyid who hadn't been born a Saliyan thought little of that country's honour, but he could understand Colonel Mahmud's feelings. Maghrebis were an emotional people, almost as revengeful as Islanders. He asked with a hint of concealed distaste:

'Then what do you intend to do?'

'God has been very good.'

'Not to the Crown He wasn't. No.'

The other two looked slightly shocked, but Mahmud ploughed on on a patriot's duty. 'All three are in one house together — the woman, Major Mortimer, Russell.'

That at least was a fact and Sayyid waited.

'We can eliminate all three at a blow.'

This time Sayyid showed disapproval for the 'eliminate' had offended and scared him. It was the word of some absurd automaton in a third-rate piece of sci-fi telly. But he recovered himself and asked politely:

'And what would be gained by that?'

'Insurance. Insurance against Russell's machinations.'

If the President had been there to hear them he might have smiled a smug smile and still been forgiven, for they were thinking as he had said they would. '*Which side is Russell on? To which side a danger?*' And they'd gone further than asking the simple questions; they had answered without even asking them. Russell was on the side of the Fox, his mere presence a proof that the Fox was employing him. They had inverted the logic of Marxist schoolboys.

But Sayyid was nursing a different objection since he thought that the phrase 'our plan' begged the question. They hadn't in fact a plan in common. The Crown and now this earnest Colonel had been thinking in terms of military action. Sayyid had never done any such thing. He had a good degree from an Ivy League college where he'd read widely outside his chosen subject, and the object of the highest strategy was not to win wars, not even blitzkriegs, but to have your ultimata accepted. You built up your power, not merely your army, till the answer to any demand must be Yes.

And he was moving within distance of that since for years he'd controlled financial policy. The Island was almost ripe for plucking. The dockyards were some sort of crazy co-operative which paid wages to the men who worked in them but little into the state's sparse coffers. The light industries were in hock to their eyeballs, kept running by the perpetual dripfeed which Saliya doled out through the House of Friendship. Only tourism was strictly profitable and with any sort of serious trouble that could dry up in a week or less. But Sayyid said nothing of this to the others.

Suleiman was making the running now, asking the questions and asking them fussily. He had the manner of a finicky don commenting on a Beta Plus essay.

'As I understand it this assassination — '

'Retribution,' Colonel Mahmud said.

'As I understand it you plan to kill all three, the two men and, since she's with them, the woman, lest they're hatching some plot which may in some way impede us. I concede that that is a sort of insurance but I'm not convinced we need pay the premium. What is the plot which you wish to insure against?'

'If I knew that I'd have another plan.'

Suleiman, the intellectual, pressed the debating point at once. 'So it's an insurance against a risk unknown.' He stole a sideways glance at Sayyid. He knew that Sayyid didn't like him but he sensed that for once they were thinking the same. They were thinking that the military ethos was no guarantee of sensible judgment.

Sayyid came in to restore the peace for this wasn't an issue to risk a break on. He realized that this had become inevitable but he intended to choose his time and place. Meanwhile he said mildly:

'Please give us the details.'

'That Greek couldn't handle a matter like this but he's good enough to have taken photographs.' Mahmud produced them, enlarged and impressive. 'That's the back of the house and that's the garden. The windows of all three bedrooms face it. And naturally we have made a mock-up.'

'You have men who could carry this out?'

'I have.' Mahmud added with a hint of impatience: 'I had men who helped with the death of the Crown.'

It was a valid point and the others nodded. 'And how are you going to get them there?'

'They will go by the ferry tomorrow evening. It arrives in the Island at eleven at night and it leaves again at six in the morning. That's plenty of time for the operation.'

'Operation?'

'Oh yes. I'd call it that.'

Sayyid said with an unconcealed disapproval: 'If I'm reading your mind they'll take more than guns.'

'The weapons they will take are dismountable. I am

sending three men which implies three suitcases. That is plenty of room for what they need and it isn't more than is comfortably carried. There's an outside chance that Customs will challenge them but the Island's officials aren't strict with Saliyans. They do not dare,' he added grimly.

'Can't you think of something less, well, sensational?' Sayyid had an upper-class horror of anything which appeared extravagant.

'Justice must be *seen* to be done.' Mahmud sounded like an Edwardian judge and in fact, though he didn't know it, was plagiarizing.

Suleiman shrugged but let it go; he hadn't the means to inhibit action. Mahmud had men and he had not. Sayyid shrugged too but for different reasons. He'd decided a struggle for power was certain but this wasn't good ground to give open battle. Nevertheless he wasn't happy. The planning was rather better than good, a sand-table exercise high in its class. Mahmud had even made a mock-up. But it was worse than a folly since wholly unnecessary.

Charles Russell was for once sleeping badly. It might have been the lobster he'd eaten, for Mediterranean lobster was suspect, or maybe it was something less lethal which was disturbing his normally placid digestion. He saw that it was three o'clock and decided on a cup of tea. He knew where everything was and he'd be quiet.

He crossed the room to fetch his dressing-gown, looking out of the window on the way. There was a neat little garden and a cool moon shone down on it. First there was a gravelled terrace, geraniums in urns on its balustrade. Below the terrace was a well-watered lawn, and this lawn sloped down to an old stone wall, the honey-coloured stone of the Island. In front of the wall was a modest folly, a miniature Ionic temple, much reduced in size but correct in scale, and each side of it four standing statues. It was a classic scene and meant to be so. Under the immaculate moon the ballet must be beginning at any time.

He went down to the kitchen and made his tea, moving carefully and not risking a light. The moon gave enough for a man with good night sight. He drank the tea and went back to his bedroom.

Half-way across it he halted abruptly. He was looking into the garden again and it wasn't a ballet, it was three purposeful men.

Instinct told him it would be unwise to be seen, so he backed till he was out of sight, working his way round the walls of the room till he stood behind the window's curtains. One man was moving across the lawn, trailing a long cable behind him. He was holding what looked like a portable searchlight. In the shadow of the Ionic folly two others were putting something together. Russell puckered his eyes. He wasn't quite up-to-date on his weaponry but he knew enough to recognize what he saw. It was a grenade launcher, quite a small one, and so would be the grenade it fired. But also it would be more than enough. One through each window and that would be final.

. . . This time they're going to make the headlines.

He turned away quickly; he must warn Robert Mortimer. But again he stopped dead where he stood for he'd heard something. It was the unmistakable cough of a silenced weapon. He waited whilst he counted two more, then moved to the window and looked again.

The man with the searchlight was sprawled beside it and the other two lay across their launcher.

Russell hesitated but made up his mind. He had overheard once and that was embarrassing: to pretend that he hadn't seen would be worse. He went to Mortimer's room and knocked. A cool voice said at once: 'Come in.'

Lucia was sitting up in bed; she seemed perfectly calm and didn't utter. Robert was cleaning a pistol meticulously.

'Pretty good shooting,' Russell said. He thought it, in the dark, remarkable. Pistol shooting had been Mortimer's hobby, an odd one for an ex-Dragoon. 'Lucky you were awake.'

'Thanks to you. You may think you move like a cat but you don't. In any case I'm a very light sleeper.' He finished cleaning the pistol and put it away. 'Let's have a look-see,' he said. 'A quick one.'

At the window he used a torch in quick flashes. 'Searchlight,' he said, 'though hardly necessary. Grenade launcher, probably Czech by the look of it. One of them for each room. . . .' He shrugged. 'And they're untidy within four walls, I assure you.'

'And what about the bodies?'

'What bodies?'

Charles Russell permitted a single quick smile. He knew now what Robert Mortimer's work was, he knew where the extra money came from. Mortimer had gone back to his trade and at it he could command a high salary. Denied a just promotion in England he had gone to another country and found it. He was saying now:

'Go back to bed, sir. Try to sleep.'

The words had the ring of unquestioned authority and Russell went back to bed at once. But not to sleep. He could hear Robert Mortimer using the telephone but he was talking in his fluent Islander. Later there was a faint noise in the garden but it was the noise of disciplined men working quietly. There was an occasional whispered order but nothing more. Russell didn't peep out since this wasn't his business, but in the morning when he got up and dressed it was seemly to look again at the garden. It was empty, there wasn't a body in sight. Nor a searchlight nor any trace of a weapon.

. . . He's gone back to his trade and he's still pretty good at it.

7

Russell was early to breakfast next morning but he found that he wasn't the first to come down. A woman was sitting and eating placidly. Russell bowed and introduced himself.

'My name's Charles Russell.'

'And mine's Concerta.'

'May I give you some more coffee?'

'Please.'

He was glad to be able to turn his back for he suspected that his face showed astonishment. She wasn't what he'd expected to find. He wouldn't have cared to define what he had, but certainly not this collected woman. She was somewhere in her early forties, buxom perhaps but by no means fat; her skin was untanned by sun and her eyes were clear. She had the manner of a contented housewife, not that of a woman who'd cut her man's head off. She was talking of the weather pleasantly. It had been hotter than usual, building up for a storm. When she'd finished her coffee he held the door for her. She gave him her comfortable smile.

'We'll meet again.'

Robert came in as Concerta left. He served himself an enormous breakfast and when he had eaten most of it said:

'I'm glad you've met Concerta at last. How did you think she was looking?'

'Well.'

'She has certainly recovered quickly. She's had a most unhappy experience.'

After last night, Charles Russell thought, he's going to recite the whole thing though I know it. It would be worse than disingenuous to conceal that I overheard him earlier.

'I know,' he said. 'I couldn't help hearing. The windows were open that night. You were shouting. Some of it was in Islander but the English bits were more than enough. I apologize as a matter of form but I don't feel in any way guilty of eavesdropping.'

'On the contrary you're making things easier. You're cutting out half the explanations because what happened last night ties up with Concerta.'

'I'm not sure I follow that.'

'It's simple. A Saliyan will see an intrigue in nothing, and in this case he did have something to go on. Concerta deprives the Crown of what wears it, an action which I deplore but can't condemn. I've been married to an Islander happily and by now I'm beginning to understand them. So Concerta kills the Crown in a temper. Naturally they've covered it up — the real story was far too hot to live with — but of course they know perfectly well she did it. And where does she run? She runs to her sister. And who is her sister? Robert Mortimer's wife, and they'll know, as you will now, that I work for the Fox. On top of that arrives Colonel Russell. He's retired but still keeps his reputation. A Saliyan would smell a plot in that, or rather since he was plotting himself what he'd smell would be a counter-plot. He wouldn't know what it was and in fact there wasn't one, but the suspicion would trigger him off into violence. Which in this case was trying to kill all three of us, Concerta, I suspect, for revenge, and you and me for what seemed the good reason that we were cooking up something which might be embarrassing. Dangerous to the Saliyan's own plans. In fact we were doing no such thing but a Saliyan wouldn't wait for proof.' The voice changed from explanation to grimness. 'One grenade for each window — they only had three. But as I told you they would have been very untidy.'

Charles Russell had listened to this without comment but there was a question which he must ask and he asked it.

'How much am I supposed to know? You told me there weren't any bodies. There were.'

'So far as the outside world is concerned I'd be grateful if you'd continue blind. But of course I've had to tell my master that you happened to see what went on last night.'

'Correctly. I'd have done the same.'

'But also, as it happens, awkwardly. The Fox would like to see you himself.'

'When would he like to?'

'Now. After breakfast.'

Charles Russell thought this a trifle cool. It would have been easy to write a polite little note, but no, he'd been summoned by oral command. He said nothing of this to Robert Mortimer but in the car he asked: 'My briefing, please.' It looked as though he would need a good one.

Robert Mortimer nodded and thought it over; finally he said deliberately:

'As I've hinted to you several times and as I'd guess you have also noticed yourself this Island is somewhat oddly run. We're not communist or a straight dictatorship but nor are we a western democracy. As examples take what happened last night but also take the late Prime Minister. He hasn't been assassinated; he was living peacefully till he had a stroke. And by the way, you're never to say 'Prime Minister'. The Fox has inherited all of his methods along with less lunatic policies, but he likes to show his independence. So his official title is Chief Executive.'

'It's a mouthful in conversation.'

'Just say "Chief".'

'And what does this Chief of yours want to talk about?'

'I think he just wants to sum you up.'

'You could have assured him of my discretion.' It was dry.

'I did and he took it. It isn't that. I think he just wants an outside opinion.'

'On the state of his country?'

'No, he knows about that. But he might ask you to assess its real danger.'

'Free?' It was even drier now.

'I dare say you could arrange a fee.'

'Not in money, I couldn't — I wouldn't even try. But as I grow older I grow more curious. It's a weakness and I confess it freely. Would he pay me in information?'

'Perhaps. But that Jesuit gave you the background.'

'Admirably. But he was also holding something back.'

'You're as shrewd as you ever were, sir.'

'I thank you. Then your Chief might spill?'

'That rather depends.'

'Depends on what?'

'It depends on whether he likes you.'

'He sounds a man to do business with.'

'Carefully.'

They were shown to the Chief Executive's office. The Chief shook hands and they all sat down. Whilst the pleasantries were being bandied Charles Russell looked round the room; he had been here before. He had been here as little more than a boy when a highly placed cousin had stood him a holiday. The furniture was still the same.

The Chief saw his puzzled look and explained. 'My predecessor was anti-British to the point that I thought him slightly insane. He cleared out all these splendid pieces and replaced them with modern Swedish rubbish. Happily they weren't destroyed, so the first thing I did was to bring them back again. I like to feel I have roots underneath me and anyway they were beautiful stuff.'

Russell nodded and waited, assessing the speaker. He had the short back and broad shoulders of Mediterranean man but his head was crowned with a shock of red hair. He had acquired it from a distant ancestor, an Orcadian seaman who had passed through the Island. Publicly he played it down but privately was intensely proud of it. He was passing his hand across it now, the affectation of a third-rate actor, but Russell could see that the gesture was natural. His teeth were still good and he showed them freely. This man might be a charlatan or again he might be something worse. Whatever he was he had flaming charisma as well as that magnificent hair.

'It was kind of you to come.'

'Not at all.'

'I asked you for more than one reason, of course. The first was to offer sincere apologies.'

Charles Russell bowed but didn't answer. The only possible answers were clichés and he guessed that he hadn't been called to exchange them.

The Fox hesitated but then said softly: 'May I ask you a personal question?'

'Certainly. But I may not answer.'

'May I take it that you're really retired?'

'If you mean did I come here to poke about? the answer is emphatically No.'

'An English journalist did.'

'I know. I met him.'

'You met him?' There was instant suspicion.

'I was having a drink in a bar and Mare walked in. I had met him before and I do not admire him. He asked me to give him a story.'

'Did you?'

'I didn't have a story to give.'

'But you've been on this Island nearly a week and you're not an unobservant man.'

. . . He would have made a very fair interrogator.

'You run your own affairs your own way. That isn't my business. Nor what Sir Perry calls a story.'

'Then our relations with a neighbouring state?'

'Are too well known to bring Perry Mare here. They're worth a think-piece in a Sunday newspaper but that isn't Sir Perry's line in journalism.'

The Chief said suddenly: 'But there *is* a story. That's why we had to throw him out.'

'You threw him out? I'd have done the same.'

'Colonel Russell, I'm beginning to like you.'

'Mutual as it happens.'

'Good. Then you'll forgive me if I talk local politics. As I hinted, we've a neighbour who covets us, but it isn't quite as simple as that. The Crown of the Faithful is dead as you know, and that the General is holding the ring pro tem.'

'Holding the ring for whom?'

'Good question. For whichever of the three men comes out top. And that is what affects this Island. The Military Member, if that's the right word for him, is all for a straight, old-fashioned invasion. The second man hardly counts and will go, but the third has a different plan. I'm sure of it.'

'Interesting.'

There was a flash of annoyance. 'You're damned detached.'

'I *am* detached. This is none of my business.'

'Would you consider a slight un-detachment?'

Charles Russell stiffened for he'd had this before. He didn't want to work for the Fox; he didn't want to work for anyone. He thought this was an indiscretion but he kept his voice as cool as ever.

'I'm afraid I wouldn't — all that is behind me. And I don't see how I could possibly help.'

'In one way you could.'

'Then you'd better tell me.'

'You nearly lost your life last night.'

Charles Russell was surprised and showed it. 'You're not suggesting I'd chatter of that?'

'I'm not suggesting, sir. Just confirming.'

'I know my host's profession and I'm his guest.' There'd been the bite of a justified irritation. Robert Mortimer frowned but he still didn't speak.

The Chief Executive rose and shook hands. 'Then all I can do is to thank you sincerely.'

They went out through the handsome airy corridor but in it they were forced to stop suddenly. A man was moving down it fast. At first he didn't appear to see them, then he suddenly waved and stopped himself. Father Gabriel said with his professional smile:

'You look surprised.'

'To see you here? Yes, in fact I am.'

'I'm afraid you're a little behind the game. The late Prime Minister was an anti-clerical and in some ways I confess I don't blame him, but the Chief hires his help where he thinks it will serve him.' He waved again at the splendid corridor. 'I've an office a little further down.'

'And interesting work?'

'Extremely. We must talk of it some time — no, on Wednesday. Have you an engagement for luncheon?'

Charles Russell shook his head.

'That's good. The restaurant at the Polly is tolerable. At half past twelve for one. Till then,' He smiled again and bustled away.

. . . Whatever he does he isn't idle.

In the car there was a minute's silence, then Mortimer said: 'So he didn't spill. At one time I really thought he was going to.'

'That reference to a story?'

'Yes.'

'Then are you going to tell me?'

'*I* don't know it. I look after what you might call the shop but I'm not in the inner ring of policy. That priest is, though, and he might tell you.'

'Why should he do that?'

'Two reasons. As you've seen he's distinctly fond of talking and he hasn't too many people to talk to. You're his equal and you're discreet by profession.'

'I'm not sure I want to hear.'

'You will.'

There was silence again till they were close to the house, then Mortimer said on a note of uncertainty: 'There's something else a little delicate.'

'Then better to spit it out in one piece.'

'It's Concerta — she's getting extremely bored. I've got my hands pretty full as you'll well imagine and Lucia has the children and housework.'

'You would like me to try to amuse her?'

'If you would.'

'What does she want to do?'

'To swim. The Crown was running scared of the sea and women were not encouraged to bathe alone.'

'I don't understand why that should be delicate. I'll take her swimming whenever she wants to go.'

More years ago than he cared to think of the General had been to a British-run Staff College, and much of what it had taught him had stuck. You put it down on paper and stared at it. As often as not what you'd written was nonsense, in which case any plan you based on it was going to be a nonsense too. He wrote in his accurate, careful English, for it was a better language to think in than Arabic. It was his private opinion, though never expressed, that if other Arab Generals would copy him the performance of their various armies might improve from what was mostly deplorable to something approaching a modest competence.

1. *I myself command a rabble. It is quite unfit to invade the Island.*

A rabble, he thought — it was not too severe. That state funeral had almost ended in scandal. An APC had been towing the gun carriage, its armoured top down, the crew at attention. And crack, it had broken the tow-rod disastrously. The driver had promptly lost his head, backing without orders to do so, overshooting and hitting the gun-carriage hard. The coffin had wobbled and almost fallen.

In recollection the General shuddered. Falling would have been shame and indignity, but suppose it had also broken open. A headless body, sheets soaked in blood. . . .

They might or might not have controlled the rioting.

And what had followed had made him wince. The cavalry had not been too bad, horsemen in their long blue cloaks, their lances at the royal salute. Militarily they were totally useless but the Crown of the Faithful had insisted on keeping them. The General had blushed at what came behind them. The armour had rolled by impressively, but the General knew it for the charade it was. The driver could just about drive and that was all. The commander stood in the open turret but he wouldn't know how to fight his vehicle. The whole Division was an expensive sham.

He shook his head to escape the memory, returning to his Appreciation.

2. *But those regiments of Mahmud are very much better, not fully trained yet but getting quite close to it. They could take the Island if ordered to do so.*

3. *But will they be given that order? That I don't know. I shall certainly never give it myself and at the moment, if given, I'd countermand it. But I may not be able to do that for long. It depends who emerges to take my place.*

The rest was too vague to be worth recording but he let himself reflect unhappily. The three Young Lions were two too many; inevitably there'd be a struggle for power. Which would come out top? He didn't know that but it wouldn't be Suleiman. Suleiman was an intellectual and it was one of nature's more merciful rules that an intellectual went first to the wall. Colonel Mahmud? That was sufficiently frightening. Mahmud had been the Crown's friend and disciple and he'd inherited his mystique and ambition. Mahmud would go for a straight invasion. Sayyid? Sayyid controlled the state's finances and Sayyid was clever as well as efficient. His plans were unknown and that was worse.

The General thought again that they'd got it wrong. Any plans for conquest were wholly lunatic when the real danger lay at home in those Guests. If they really got out of hand they could topple the state.

He was interrupted by an orderly. 'The Chief of Staff is waiting outside, sir.'

'Then show him in at once.'

He came in and saluted, extremely dapper. The General

might command a rabble but he could keep his personal staff clean and soldierly.

'Good morning. Sit down. What can I do for you?'

'Come and look if you will. There's trouble in the city again.'

'Our Guests, I suppose.'

'The usual thing. Banners saying GIVE US OUR RIGHTS, placards saying THE RATE FOR THE JOB Chanting and some sporadic stone-throwing.'

'Why should I come for that? It's normal.'

'Because the police have lost control. They're firing and they're firing volleys.'

'Into the crowd?' This was bad indeed.

'No, over their heads.'

This was very much worse. The General was very angry and showed it, his meticulous training outraged and offended. They had taken him on an Exercise called 'Aid to the Civil Power and its Pitfalls' and the Instructor had been firm and explicit. Firing over the heads of crowds was forbidden in the Book of Words and forbidden for an excellent reason. It didn't frighten them but it made them more hostile. In any case firing was out without orders and those orders must come from a civil authority. Be very careful indeed to get them and make sure that they were properly signed. If you could get them witnessed so much the better but legally you couldn't insist on that. The point was that you *must* get your order. It was all that stood between you and Court Martial for the civilians would let you down if they could, especially in an Asian country. With that on your tail you'd be finished for ever.

So you got your order first and then thought: you weren't out of the wood yet, you *needed* to think. For the doctrine now was 'Minimal Force'. The crowd might be smelly and subsidized students, spitting at you, throwing bags of excrement, but you weren't allowed to brown them down. That had been done in India once and the man who had done it had not been forgiven. So pick a couple of targets and drop them, then back to your Magistrate . . . 'Is that enough, sir?' If he says Yes you are back in the clear, but if he says No get another order or at least two reliable men who heard him. Remember that he isn't your comrade; he'll drop you in the dirt if he can. And remember above all things in heaven never to fire over anyone's head.

The General stood up at once. 'I'll come.'

As they neared the central square they heard it, the unmistakable noise of an angry crowd. The Chief of Staff used the staff car's radio.

'The police have been driven back to the palace. They're inside now and it seems still firing.'

'Fools,' the General said.

'What now?'

'Has the palace a back entrance?'

'Surely.'

'Drive to it at once. And fast.'

A policeman was on guard and saluted. He did it sloppily and was dressed like a scarecrow.

'Get that man's name. He's a national disgrace.'

They went through the deserted palace, finding their way up stairs and through corridors till they reached the front which faced the square. A fine balcony overlooked it imperiously and on it were a handful of policemen. They looked frightened and indeed they were.

The General said: 'Cease fire. At once.'

He took in the situation quickly since it wasn't very hard to read it. This kind of disturbance had happened before but it hadn't been exacerbated by gunfire. The crowd was furious — worse, it was confident. If this was the worst the police could do. . . .

The General took it in at once but he felt himself between the horns. Instinct and training pulled different ways. His instinct was to fire at will, to teach a lesson to these impertinent aliens, but he couldn't do that, his Instructor would fail him. In the end he went back to the Book — it was safest. He took off his belt, his cap and his jacket, throwing them to a policeman who muffed it. They fell on the dusty cement and the General cursed. He said to the Chief of Staff:

'Observe me. I am now a civilian. I'm the head of this state though I didn't seek it, and as such I am going to give you orders.'

The puzzled Brigadier said: 'Yes, sir?'

'Have you a message pad?'

'Yes, of course.'

He passed it and the General wrote, this time from right to left, in Arabic. The Chief of Staff read the message and stared. 'Your instructions are to restore good order?'

'That's what I'd intended to write.'

'But how?'

The General wasn't pleased; he exploded. 'Good God, man, that isn't my business now. I'm the civil power and I call you in aid.'

The Chief of Staff was out of his depth but he looked at the roaring crowd below them. There was a man on a soap-box calling the chants.

'He looks like the leader.'

'That's your business now. Do I have to feed you your mother's milk? Those policemen there have rifles, haven't they?'

'Unhappily I'm not a marksman.'

'You should be able to hit a man at fifty yards.'

The Chief of Staff took a weapon uncertainly. It was years since he'd fired a service rifle and it hadn't a telescopic sight. But the balance was good, the stock fitted his shoulder. He knelt down behind the balustrade, resting the rifle across its top. He loaded with a single shot; he took the first pressure and then the second. The cheerleader fell off his box untidily.

Instantly there was frightened silence. The crowd had begun to retreat, first slowly, then accelerating into a panic scramble. Two men were towing the cheerleader by his legs.

The Chief got up from his knees rather stiffly. He took

out the magazine with care, then he worked the bolt and blew down the barrel. All this was a wholly reflex drill, as deep in his veins as the blood which ran in them. He handed the rifle back to the policeman.

The General began to dress disgustedly. His jacket was crumpled, his cap was a mess. Finally he slipped into his belt. It hadn't a cross strap but two in parallel, one across each shoulder, vertical, like the British regiment he'd served six months with. He was hot and dirty, he felt like a scarecrow, but secretly he was happy, at peace. He'd kept all the rules though perhaps he'd bent them. Well, circumstances altered cases. That Instructor of his would have passed him high.

Behind them the square was entirely empty. 'Back to headquarters,' he said. 'And tread on it.'

They went through the neglected corridors, down the staircase to the palace back door. The police sentry was still propping it open.

'Show me your weapon.'

He brought it up carelessly.

'You're dirty and slack, a disgrace to the Police Force.'

They got into their car and drove away.

The General lit a reflective cigar. . . . That had been an easy one, just a matter of keeping the rules he'd been taught, but the next one could be much more serious. That crowd had been the President's citizens, unorganized and unarmed, just protesting. Protesting against a plain injustice with which the General had much sympathy privately. But if the President chose to send them real leaders he could enforce his demands if he happened to have any or alternatively he could wreck Saliya.

The fuse would burn on until somebody doused it and how to do that he didn't know. Or rather he did but the Lions wouldn't let him.

8

The General, if he'd known what was happening, would not have been wholly surprised to hear it. He'd been certain that the Young Lions would fight, but he hadn't expected the power struggle quite so soon.

Nevertheless the battle had opened. Mahmud was sitting in Sayyid's flat and neither was sure of the other's response. Mahmud was trying to talk classical Arabic and Sayyid was hiding the fact that it made him wince. But it was the perfect language for innuendo, for withdrawing at once if you'd gone too far.

'I have the impression that Your Honour is troubled.'

'I have the same feeling of you, My Brother.'

'Our Country faces difficult days.'

'Our Beloved Country will face them victoriously.'

'The Almighty wills it.'

'Be sure of that.'

The opening moves had been made with propriety and both of them became slightly less flowery. 'Our General— ' Mahmud began.

'A fine man.'

'Can he hold the situation?'

'Do we really want him to?'

This was going a little too fast for Mahmud who began to put the brakes on at once. 'We must accept God's will.'

'His Will could change.'

Colonel Mahmud could see that Sayyid meant business.

The sparring was over, the chips were down. So he waited for Sayyid's next move. It came.

'The alternative to rule by the General is rule by ourselves as a kind of *troika*.'

'Which we cannot yet claim, far less enforce.'

'And a *troika* is a clumsy vehicle.'

Mahmud didn't answer this but walked to the window and looked out of it silently. He knew Sayyid was extremely rich, he'd salted money away in more countries than Switzerland, but in Saliya ostentation was frowned on and the Crown himself had lived very quietly. So Sayyid lived in this concrete block in a suburb and Mahmud stared at the beach which it overlooked. There was a strip of tarmac promenade and on it men were pacing gravely. Some wore the dress of their race with dignity, others wore European clothes. Especially the Guests wore coat and trousers. Mahmud hated them but he knew they were necessary. And whatever their race the men walked without protest, indifferent to the ravished beach. Swimming wasn't a popular Arab pastime and the beach had become a poor man's loo. Sometimes the sea cleaned the turds, sometimes not, and when it did not the stench was appalling. But none of these solemnly pacing figures seemed even aware that a nuisance existed.

Mahmud returned and repeated: 'A *troika*.'

'As I said, it's an unwieldy vehicle.'

They now understood each other perfectly. Two regiments of well-trained infantry was a power base by any accounting known, and so was control of the state corporation which in turn ran such oil as the Crown chose to leave it. But Intelligence was no base whatever. It was important and Suleiman ran it competently, but in the pinches one could do without it, at any rate for the first days of crisis. Intelligence was expendable, *ergo* Suleiman was himself expendable.

Besides, neither of the other two liked him. He put on his little airs and graces which Mahmud, the soldier, resented sharply, and Sayyid who'd seen the West in its decadence had learnt its lessons and thought him ridiculous. He was wet and he had progressive ideas, the body odour of liberal humanism. He was a professional compassioner, he was interested in prison reform. If he had his way he'd enfranchise the Guests; he might even allow the ultimate horror, the establishment of effective trade unions. Sayyid was an upper-crust Arab and he regarded all or any of these as disasters to be avoided at all costs. He said to Mahmud but very softly:

'Could you run Intelligence?'

'You'd do it better.'

It was the polite, the expected thing to say and Mahmud had batted it back by instinct. But it was also true and Sayyid knew it. Mahmud had his own fish to fry, those parachute regiments which would never be used. Sayyid was perfectly sure of that. So long as the General held the ring the Island would not be taken by force. He had his own plan for that and moreover a better one. But he didn't allow the thought to form sharply. Mahmud was an Arab too, which meant that he was also perceptive.

Perceptive enough to have read the main message. 'Two,' he said quietly, 'would be better than one.'

'I'm delighted we see alike.'

'We do.' They were out in the open now, talking freely. Colonel Mahmud asked: 'And the practical side?'

'Could you arrange it yourself?'

'Unless you wish to take it on.'

'I think you have better facilities.'

'Probably.'

'Then God go with you.'

'We're in His Hands.'

When Mahmud had gone Sayyid poured a whisky. It was illegal but he had means to acquire it. He was far from a soak but liked a drink in the evening, the only form of western degeneracy which he didn't consider entirely deplorable. He poured three fingers of rye and sipped them.

He had a real respect for Colonel Mahmud since he had virtues which he hadn't himself, but one couldn't deny that the man was provincial. He was committed and loyal but his loyalty blinded him. The Crown had been his friend and idol and now he would guard the arcana with his life. But the death of the Crown had changed everything drastically. Mahmud hadn't seen that and he never would. The King is dead, his ambitions with him. One of them had been remarkably foolish, but Mahmud would go on pursuing it stubbornly till it brought him to a head-on collision with the General who thought it foolish too. Mahmud would overreach himself and the penalty for that was final. Dedication was much more dangerous than whisky.

Sayyid finished his modest drink and went to bed. Two was better than three but one would be best. Particularly one with the same objective but a sane political plan to achieve it.

The Island plugged its beaches remorselessly but in fact they were very poor indeed, mostly in inaccessible places, small and often sullied by oil from the stream of tankers which passed north and south of them. But the bathing from rock was superb if you liked it, straight down into deep water at once.

Charles Russell had kept his promise to Mortimer and had let Concerta choose the place. She hadn't insisted on somewhere isolated but had taken him to a quiet establishment. It had a platform with deck chairs and mattresses and a small but very attentive bar. He hadn't spoken with her often before but they had slipped into an easy relationship. She wasn't a woman who talked very much but the little she said had the tang of good ale. Together they could both relax comfortably.

They had finished their swimming and she'd swum very strongly. Now she was on a mattress, prone, and Russell in a chair drinking gin. She wore an old-fashioned one-piece swimsuit which showed off her full figure magnificently.

A Rubens would have spat on his hands. Russell didn't do this but he wasn't blind, nor insensitive to the fact that she liked him.

'I missed that in Saliya,' she said.

'So Robert told me.'

'He told you right. Sometimes you could slip away but you had to go a long way to do it and you had to take another woman. I hadn't many women friends.'

It was an opening but he passed it up. Instead he said: 'I know what happened.'

'You do? I'm delighted. It saves explanations.'

'I wasn't going to ask for any.'

'No, you don't look the type.'

'A very nice compliment.'

They fell into a companionable silence, then Concerta said: 'I don't know what I'm going to do here.'

'You were happy in Saliya?'

'Contented. I had a man I rather liked who was generous. Or he was till the end when he dropped me flat.'

'You were lucky to get away.'

'I was. But I left everything I had behind me. I had some money saved but the bank has that. I suppose you don't think I could get it out?'

'I'm afraid I think it is most improbable.'

'So what am I going to do on this Island? I can't live for ever as Robert's pensioner.'

'You might start another shop,' he said.

'I suspect that you're pulling my leg unkindly. You'll know that the shop I kept was a butcher's. Arabs will accept the bizarre provided it's not their own women who do it, and in any case I was the only good butcher. But on this conventional, hidebound rock I'd go broke within a week. Probably there's a law against it too.'

'You could marry,' he said. 'You're extremely attractive.'

'A murderess?'

'Who's to know?'

She laughed at him. 'You're very English. In this dull

little dump there's no such thing as a secret. Everything gets out in time.'

'You'd still be married.'

'But on what sort of terms? I need a man but not a master, and once he'd found out I'd be nailed to the floor.'

Charles Russell nodded; he thought her right. 'Shall we swim again?'

'A short one this time.'

Charles Russell went down the ladder gently but Concerta dived in in a fine bold arc. He noticed again that she swam superbly. He was at home in the water himself and loved it but he wasn't in this woman's class.

They returned to the platform. 'Another drink?'

'Not for the moment, thank you.'

'All right.' He looked at his watch. 'Then I'll take you to luncheon.'

To his astonishment she turned away. For some reason unknown she was hiding her face. When she'd recovered she faced him frankly. 'You don't have to do that,' she said at last.

'Why ever not?' He was still at a loss.

'Well,' she said, 'you know — '

'Oh that!' He was distinctly annoyed that she thought him conventional.

'You really want me to come?'

'I asked you, didn't I?'

'You're a very nice man.' She took off her cap and shook her hair; she was suddenly several years younger and gay. 'Then where shall we go?'

'I've heard that the Polly — '

'It's a little bit grand.'

'It'll do to start with.'

'I know that it's changed hands of late. Swiss management and Italian food.'

'An excellent combination,' he said.

She looked at him without a flicker. 'I can think of a better.'

'Ask me again.'

She wasn't offended but smiled an acknowledgement. 'Then I'll go and change.'

'Don't take too long.'

Suleiman had been rather lucky for Arabs weren't always good with explosives. They might have blown off his legs and left him a cripple but this time they'd used an adequate charge. He climbed into his car and considered since he'd only just learnt to drive and was careful, deliberate by natural habit and with the intellectual's passion for trifles. He turned the key half-way till the red light showed. Excellent — the circuits were working. Then he turned it all the way and died. There was an instant of blinding pain, then oblivion. The fire engine took an hour to arrive and by that time there was a smoking ruin.

When the General heard he pulled his moustache. He had expected violence but not quite so soon. Now that it had come he accepted it. He thought as Sayyid had thought, identically. Two Young Lions were better than three. By one Young Lion.

9

Father Gabriel had asked him to luncheon next day and Charles Russell arrived at the Polly punctually. But punctual as he was the priest had beaten him. He was sitting in the smaller bar drinking what looked like a large pink gin. He caught Russell's look of surprise and said:

'A habit I acquired in the Navy. How do you take your own?'

'With tonic. And I didn't know you'd been in the Navy.'

'Why should you? I rated as a steward, you see.' It was said with the faintest hint of resentment. 'It's one of an Islander's traditional employments. I made Captain's Steward and that was the lot.'

'You must have been good at the job.'

'I was.'

They went into the dining-room and the waiter produced two impressive menus. Russell gave his own the barest glance. 'The sole,' he said, 'is quite first class.'

'You have been here before?'

'I lunched here yesterday. With a lady, Mortimer's sister-in-law.'

The priest said: 'You've a very strong stomach.'

'With respect to your cloth I think that's nonsense. I know she chopped off her lover's head but to do it she used the tools of her trade. The action was perfectly seemly and apposite. A woman doctor would have poisoned him and a croquet player bashed his head in.'

The Jesuit choked on his wine but recovered. 'My Order would have accepted you gladly.'

'I doubt it but I accept the compliment.'

They ate for some time in an easy silence till Father Gabriel said: 'I thought you looked surprised to see me. At the Chief Executive's office, I mean.'

'I was but I think I've worked it out. You belong to an international Order, you have eyes and ears in most countries on earth. Even in Saliya itself it's not yet illegal to be a Christian. You don't get far if you are one, true, but there's no active or overt persecution.'

'And what do you deduce from that?'

'I deduce that you run the Fox's Intelligence.'

'Perfectly correct. Full marks.'

'So you've asked me to lunch as a colleague — ex-colleague?'

'Not quite correct but pretty close. I know that you wouldn't help — you've no motive to — but I'd very much welcome a second opinion.'

'I might give it at a price.'

'What price?'

'Information. Without it any opinion is valueless.'

'That's reasonable. And reassuring. You haven't lost the habits which made you.' Father Gabriel broke off to order pie and a salad. 'I think I once told you the Fox was no fool. The late Prime Minister was, a big one. He talked about building a bridge between east and west. That was a pipe-dream and the Chief has abandoned it. All the Fox wants is strict neutrality, and in the proper sense of the word he pretends to it. He won't get it of course, but I still pray he will.'

'Why shouldn't he get it?'

'The rules of *realpolitik*. A state of this size can only be neutral on one of two conditions, neither fulfilled. The first is a credible military force and the second a powerful guarantor. Evidently we don't have the first but the Fox has been trying to find the second. NATO won't do, they can manage without us, and the Prime Minister pushed them too far for recovery. So the Fox tried the French and they turned him down. There wasn't any visible gain to offset the very obvious dangers. He even tried a second Arab state. They laughed at him.'

'Did they indeed? That rather surprises me.'

'Why?' Father Gabriel was suddenly as sharp as a razor.

'If I was understanding you rightly when we were talking before your present danger comes from Saliya. And if we're talking about the same second state it is not on very good terms with its neighbour.'

'I agree that relations are pretty strained. But not as strained as all that. Not yet.'

'Obviously you know more than I do.'

'But you're perfectly right about Saliya.' The priest attacked his salad with gusto. It was a good crisp salad and he ate it noisily. 'Have you heard of the Three Young Lions?'

'A little. Mortimer gave me the basic outline and your Chief was dropping hints when I met him. There's what you might call a military wing and another which you could call civilian. Where the third man stands I do not know.'

'He doesn't stand, he's as dead as the Crown. His car blew up with himself inside it.'

'You do not surprise me. They're that sort of people.'

'Nevertheless it's a simplification.'

'Then which way are you betting — civil or military?'

'I'm betting on the civil strongly.'

'May I ask why?'

'I invited you here to tell you that.' A moment's hesitation, then: 'Have you heard of the Median Line?'

'What's that? Median, I suppose, means half-way.'

'Just so. It's the half-way line between ourselves and Saliya and it runs slap through what may be a major oil-field.'

'So that's the story your Fox wouldn't tell me, the reason you threw out Mare so promptly. He's a horrible man but he does have a nose.' Charles Russell in turn took a mouthful of salad. 'I saw a survey ship in the harbour once. She flew the Dutch flag and your own and Saliya's. I thought that a little odd at the time.'

'She's operating for both of us jointly and we earnestly hope that enormous wages will keep the hand-picked crew secure. For apart from the crew and now yourself only three men know that oil has been found — the Chief, myself and the civilian Young Lion. He's called Sayyid, by the way, and he's clever.'

'With oil at stake he will need to be clever.'

'I don't like that "at stake" at all.'

'But surely if it runs through the middle — '

'Any normal man would think like that but international lawyers aren't normal. There are capes and promontories, shelves — God knows what. Already we're disputing secretly and that doesn't ease what's already strained.'

'You could go to the International Court.'

'If that was a joke it was rather a sour one. We'd need to bribe our way to a narrow majority and I doubt if we can afford their prices. In any event if we won our case Saliya would simply ignore the judgment.' The voice fell into sarcastic quotes. ' "If any party to a case fails to adhere to the judgment of the Court, the other party may have recourse to the Security Council." And you'll know as well as I do what that means. Saliya could get any action blocked easily. That takes even more money. Saliya has it.'

'Then what are you intending to do?'

'Negotiate till they put the real screws on. They're greedy and they want the whole of it.'

'They have some of their own already.'

'True. But you forget that they are also Arabs.'

'You think they'll try to take you over?'

'Not by force, or not by force directly. If what the Chief called the military member knew — Mahmud is his name, by the way — there'd probably be some violent action. But my information is that he doesn't know. Sayyid is playing this one personally and Sayyid is very much smarter than Mahmud. Smarter and therefore much more dangerous.'

'What can Sayyid do?'

The Jesuit reflected coolly. 'Naturally I don't know his plan but he could put us in some hopeless position where we'd have to accept his terms and capitulate. With that would go our half of the oil and everything that oil might have meant to us.'

'What could he really do in fact?'

Father Gabriel seemed to be changing the subject. 'Have you ever been to the suburb of Xalah?'

'As it happens I have and I didn't like it.'

'Too many Saliyans?'

'And not very nice ones. I gather they come for drink and women.'

'But they're still Saliyans.'

'Oh, lay it down straight.'

Father Gabriel smiled but he didn't decline. 'There's still one excuse for intervention which the modern world accepts fairly happily. If a state maltreats your own people you may act. The French did it not long ago in Africa and only the far, far Left raised an eyebrow. Not that I think they'd use their paratroops, or they won't if Sayyid wins against Mahmud, but give Sayyid an excuse and he'll use it.'

The coin had dropped but only half-way. 'If those Saliyans rioted it wouldn't help Sayyid. You'd be entitled to put down a riot in your country.'

The Jesuit smiled his blandest smile. 'I don't think you're with me.'

'That's uncomfortably true.'

'Then I wasn't considering rioting Saliyans. I was considering Islanders rioting against them.'

'Why should they do that?'

'Some insult. Some wrong which they thought the Saliyans had done them. We're a violent and hot-headed people.'

The penny had gone the whole distance now. 'But that

wrong would have to be fixed — set up.'

'Are you telling me it couldn't be?'

'No.'

Father Gabriel finished his pie with appetite. 'Be it in Xalah or be it elsewhere "excuse" is the word which really matters. Give Sayyid that and I don't doubt he'll act.'

'What do you think he'll do?'

'I told you that — send an ultimatum. He doesn't want this infertile rock, he doesn't believe in Arab imperialism. What he wants is that oil and he means to have it. So down comes the ultimatum — bang. Abandon any claim to that oil or I'll pull the economic rug out. Remember he'd have an excuse to do so. Not a perfect one but he'd know how to use it. The Arab world would be solid behind him and the Arab world holds the West where it hurts.'

'What would happen if he pulled out the rug?'

'Do you know what we owe them?' He named a figure. 'Demand the first and stop the second and we'd be starving in a couple of months. Nobody would much care if we did — the late Prime Minister saw to that. He put all our eggs in a single basket and now we're a very soft omelette indeed.'

They went to the Polly's veranda for coffee. It overlooked the smaller harbour. Across the water was the ancient lazar house, crumbling but still with elegant lines. To the left was Robert Mortimer's suburb, half hidden by a newer hospital. Two tourist launches were chugging peacefully. The sun shone down from a cloudless sky.

Father Gabriel said: 'I love my country.'

An Englishman would not have said it but in this Islander's mouth it was perfectly seemly.

'That I can see. But enough to leave your Order?'

'I haven't. I'm on a sort of detachment — sabbatical leave. My Superior didn't like it much, but then, you see, he's an Islander too.'

'He sounds an intelligent man.'

'Of course.'

They sat silently, soaking the splendid scene in. Presently

the priest said softly:

'Does this Island bewitch you? It does some Englishmen.'

'I like it. I wouldn't say bewitch.'

'Enough to help us?'

'Not enough.'

'I'm sorry but I'm not despairing. I make guesses which a good priest shouldn't and my guess is that before you leave us some Islander will do you a kindness. Which, being what you are, you'll repay.'

'It could happen, I suppose.'

'It will.'

He had said that they wouldn't come by force but half an hour later his faith was shaken. Father Gabriel had gone to his office to nap but was woken by the clatter of helicopters. He went out to his balcony, unbelieving. They seemed to be very low and dropping. . . . Mother of God, they were going to buzz them. Two were much too low, though still safe, but the third had come very low indeed.

On the other side of the fine old courtyard the Chief was on his balcony too. He was shouting though his voice was inaudible and waving his arms in furious gestures. The third chopper came even lower still. The priest could see the pilot's face but his helmet inhibited recognition. It was split in a goblin grin of hatred.

The blast of the blades blew the Jesuit down but he pulled himself upright and clung to the railing. The Chief Executive had disappeared but Father Gabriel stayed on a sullen defiance. The flag had been torn from its mast in shreds, the shrubs in the courtyard cruelly flattened. Tiles had begun to fly, first singly, then, from one side, in a lethal shower. A woman had been running for cover and she dropped on her face and lay unmoving. Windows had been blown inwards brutally; the dust rose in a blinding, choking swirl.

It settled slowly as the aircraft rose and Father Gabriel ran to the Fox's office. He was sitting at his desk, writing fast. He handed the paper over.

'Have that sent at once.'

'I will.'

It was a formal protest but not written formally, a natural expression of natural anger. In his office the priest slightly toned it down but he left it as what the Fox intended, the expression of an offended outrage.

Colonel Mahmud was half-way across the sea when he realized he'd done something unpardonable. He'd been flying the leading chopper himself for he had earned his wings and liked to use them. They had been in the Island's air space legitimately, photographing such NATO shipping as still, if reluctantly, used the harbour. This they were entitled to do by arrangement with the late Prime Minister. The Fox had considered cancellation but he knew that he'd pay a price if he dared it. Some project would be promptly abandoned, say that shoe factory he'd set his heart on. The shoes wouldn't compete with those from Italy but the factory would give welcome work to may be three hundred men who supported him. If they didn't they'd find that the work somehow missed them.

So Mahmud's flight had been flying legitimately but Mahmud had been in a very bad temper. He had lost three good men in a profitless sortie and that weighed heavily on his soldier's conscience. The man Russell was still alive and menacing. He did not love the land below him.

His observer was working the camera busily and Mahmud had leisure to look around him. To the south he could see the Inquisitor's palace. Unspeakable things had happened there and mostly they had happened to Islanders. But not exclusively to Islanders. No. His own people had been crippled and burned, thrown into underground prisons and starved. He muttered in a rising anger, then looked to the north and suddenly stiffened. For there it was and flying still, the Great Cross. He knew that the building from which it flew was now no more than a fourth-rate embassy, one from a Power which no longer existed except in one smallish house in Rome; he knew that the Islanders smiled in their sleeves at it. Nevertheless that flag was an insult. The men whose badge it was were dishonoured. Mahmud shared Charles Russell's opinion. For all this panoply of arms and bearings the Order didn't behave like gentlemen. Gentlemen kept their given word; they didn't go out and enslave one's ancestors. Mahmud had two who had died in their galleys.

It was intolerable that this two-fart Island should permit such a show of shameless dishonour. For what was this arrogant rock? It was nothing. Its rulers strutted the stage in motley, babbling of political bridges. Its politicians were puppets, clownish Pretenders. Its forces couldn't quieten a girls' school, far less determined men from the sky. The Island had been Arab once and to a man as stubborn as Colonel Mahmud it was going to be Arab again if he died for it. He owed that to his late master, the Crown.

He picked up the radio, calling the other two. 'We're going to buzz the Fox's office.'

An astonished voice said: 'Say again.'

'You heard me the first time. Follow me.'

But half-way back to his base in Saliya Mahmud realized he'd done something serious, and whether he could meet his bill would depend on a single man, the General.

Who was reading the Fox's protest carefully for the firmness of its terms surprised him. It was still within diplomacy's limits, not something which he could refuse to accept, but it was the language of perfectly genuine anger. The General was inclined to sympathize. To buzz a Chief Executive's office, to break windows and strip tiles from a roof were the acts of an irresponsible lunatic, and one of the flying tiles had killed. There was an express demand for compensation and that would have to be met in decency; there was also one for a full apology and this would have to be granted too; finally there was one for punishment and the General knew that this might be difficult. If an officer had been flying that chopper the General's power to discipline openly was limited by the political fact that if his junior officers took it badly there'd be complications which might lead him anywhere.

He sent a holding answer in the politest of terms — an inquiry was being started immediately — then telephoned for his Chief of Staff. He showed him the message dourly.

'Well?'

'I'll make a full inquiry at once.'

The Chief of Staff came back in an hour. He was a humourless man and reported humourlessly. 'At the time which that protest gives for the incident no naval helicopter was off the ground. The army proper has only a handful and these I have accounted for carefully. Neither of them was near the Island. On the other hand Colonel Mahmud's two regiments have been fully equipped for landings by air.'

'Have you made inquiries of Colonel Mahmud?'

'No sir. I thought that I should speak to you first.'

The simple statement said more than the words. Mahmud and his superior regiments were formally under the General's command but it was a command which he dare not lean on too heavily. The Chief of Staff had known this too and the General thought he had acted wisely. But he couldn't simply let this one go.

'Send for Mahmud, please. I want him at once.'

He spent the interval in uneasy thought for he preferred his problems clear-cut and decidable and this one was almost certainly neither. Unless his Chief of Staff was mistaken, and the General thought that very unlikely, it could only have been one of Mahmud's officers who'd been flying as only a fool would fly. Mahmud's officers were a *corps d'élite* and the men they led well trained and well armed. The ordinary army greatly outnumbered them but the General knew that he couldn't rely on it. He knew it would be insane to do so. The General had armour and Mahmud hadn't, but he thought again of the late Crown's funeral, of the near disasters of poorly trained men, of the tanks which had rolled by impressively, one in ten of them barely fit for action.

And if it came to action would they act? The General couldn't be sure of that. Mahmud's two regiments were not yet Israelis but they were coming up to a comparable standard, the cream of the country's men with the best of its arms. That had been the Crown's own policy and by now the General couldn't reverse it. Mahmud had been the Crown's favourite son and a dutiful son had accepted his legacy, a wild plan to seize the Island by force. The General had always thought that misguided, but the means to do so had been built up deliberately, two fine regiments which were improving daily. His own men were well fed and contented; they wouldn't turn against him easily. But whether they would fight in his interest was a question he couldn't answer with certainty.

He'd need more than his General Officer's badges to handle this problem without a crisis.

He heard a staff car stop on the gravel outside and went to the window to watch what happened. Mahmud got out and his driver saluted. The driver was in shirtsleeve order but clean and very much a soldier. Mahmud was in service dress and the General found that vaguely disturbing, an omen of some expected formality. Outside in the sun it was a hundred and thirty.

He went back to his desk and Mahmud knocked.

'Come in,' the General said.

Mahmud came. He was pressed and polished as though for inspection, wearing his belt with a conscious elegance. It was black with silver buckles, a compromise, but it emphasized what the General knew, that he commanded two regiments which thought themselves special. Certainly his salute was special. He did it very smartly indeed.

'You wanted me, sir?'

'I did. Sit down.'

The General handed Mahmud the protest. 'I have established that it was one of your helicopters.'

'Yes sir, I'm afraid it was.'

'Disgraceful. The name of the officer, please.'

'I was flying it myself that day.'

A silence, then angrily: 'Why did you do it?'

'I'm sorry to say I lost my head.'

There was another long silence through which the General sat motionless. He had trained his face not to show his thoughts but this blow had caught him unprepared. It was bad enough that in the state of Saliya there were two Divisions of a doubtful standard and what amounted to a private army of competence which was increasing daily. Formally he commanded both but the private army had political backing. Its commander had been the Crown's friend and confidant and he was still very much one of two Young Lions. Not a happy position for any General, one without ambition politically, one who was holding the country together until someone appeared with the strength to take over.

All this, then, was bad enough as it stood, but when the commander of this private army committed an inexcusable outrage the horns of the General's dilemma had sharpened. On the one hand was the real risk of a *coup*, that if he relieved this superbly dressed man of command he might be tempted into some further foolishness which the General wasn't sure he could meet and which might tear the unstable state to pieces; on the other the humiliation of acting with less than proper firmness.

He made up his mind but he did so reluctantly. 'Colonel,' he said, 'you are reprimanded. The reprimand will go on your record.'

When Mahmud had gone he looked at the Note again. It demanded an apology. Certainly. It demanded compensation. It would be paid. It also demanded that those concerned should be suitably dealt with and he knew that they hadn't been.

Nevertheless his humiliation was tempered by a certain pride. He had acted in his country's interests and for a reason of which he was wholly convinced. Any plans to seize the Island were nonsense, or rather they were misdirected. It was absurd to dream of imperialist expansion from a base which was threatened inside itself. Threatened by Our Guests and increasingly.

The General had always put that first and after the riot he was surer than ever. It was true that they'd suppressed it quite easily, but for the first time there'd been an identifiable leader and the General thought that distinctly ominous. He'd been shot but another would take his place. Another and perhaps a better. If they really got together, organized, they could hold the state to effective ransom. And it wasn't inconceivable that their own state would assist them actively. In which case there'd be an open war, in which case he'd need every man he'd got including Mahmud's private army.

He allowed himself a single wry smile. He'd been pleased when the Crown had made him a General and he'd realized why he himself had been chosen: he was safe and loyal and a little old-fashioned; he wasn't a political animal. And here he was in the great snake's coils, fighting battles which he'd never expected, battles he hadn't been trained to fight.

He sighed for he wasn't a happy man. He'd intended to spend the week-end at his villa where his roses would need his loving attention. There was a gardener but he over-watered. The roses, left to him, would be weeds.

He pushed himself up from his chair with his hands. He felt suddenly very old and tired.

But Mahmud drove back to his camp contented for the morning had confirmed to him something which he had long suspected. That something was that the General feared him. The word was frank but it wasn't too strong. If the positions had in fact been reversed, if he'd been a General and the General the culprit, he'd have relieved him of his command on the spot, very possibly court martialled him too. But the General had done neither of these. A reprimand had been nothing, evident eyewash.

He considered the implications coolly. 'Feared' was perhaps an overstatement but 'would tread warily' was surely not. And in a couple of weeks he'd be ready to move.

He took the master plan from his safe and flicked the pages. A great deal of patient work had gone into it quite apart from the training of men to carry it out. Whatever he'd asked for the Crown had given him, the most modern equipment, the best of everything. Only one thing was lacking now, the certainty that there wasn't some counter-plan, some trap into which his men might stumble. For Russell was still on the Island intriguing.

His conscious mind flashed a conscious message — aren't you making altogether too much of him? — but instinct suppressed the import instantly. Was there not plenty to go on? Yes there was. Why had Charles Russell arrived in the first place? And the Greek had been sending a stream of snippets. Russell had been to see the Fox and, worse, he'd had lunch with that scheming priest. Something was brewing — it must be brewing — but Mahmud couldn't guess what it was. Bring back the British secretly? They wouldn't come. NATO? It wouldn't dare to act. The French perhaps? Not so long ago they had owned the place and they'd recently proved that they still had teeth, the means and the will to act unilaterally. Whatever it was he was certain of one thing: Charles Russell was at the heart and core of it. Which made him the immediate danger.

A fortnight, he thought again — fourteen days. Intolerable to see his life's work broken when he could insure it by the death of Russell. He'd tried once before and lost three good men. This time he would do it himself.

He looked at another snippet from the Greek. Charles Russell and that woman Concerta went bathing together and did so regularly. They did it from the Rabbit's Neck which was well to the south of the Island and lonely. They arrived about ten and went in at ten-thirty.

. . . Both of them together. Tempting. Russell to buy himself time he thought vital, Concerta an acceptable bonus, the woman who'd murdered his friend and patron.

It wouldn't be easy, there were serious difficulties, but he believed he could find a road around them. After all he was a very fair pilot.

Charles Russell had hired a car to go swimming and when they'd swum he drove Concerta home. They had lunch and Charles Russell went upstairs for his nap. When he came down she gave him tea and a sealed envelope of very thick paper. On the back was a blazon Charles Russell remembered. 'When did this come?' he asked.

'About three. It was brought by a well-spoken young Arab. He wanted me to wake you at once but I wouldn't do that and he wasn't pleased. In the end we made a sort of compromise. I promised you shouldn't leave the house till I'd seen you actually read the letter.'

It was typed again and again unsigned.

I warned you once before and you paid no attention. Now I know I was right and so do you. They seem to have got very close to killing you. I beg you to go to my embassy. Now.

'From a girl-friend?' Concerta asked with a smile. She was curious and saw no reason to hide it.

'Hardly that. The writer is a friend of mine who's conceived the idea that he's in my debt. From his point of view I suppose he is but from mine the whole affair is a nuisance. I don't want repayment — I've never thought of it.'

She said in her simple earthy manner: 'A useful friend to have. A bit in the bank.'

'It would be if I could draw on the account. As it is there's nothing I want from this friend and I can't imagine there ever will be.'

'Don't be too sure of that.'

'Why not?'

'Just call it an intuition.'

'I will.'

He put the note in his pocket to think it over but he knew

that he'd made up his mind already. Evidently Mr President had excellent sources of information but Russell was rather less than sure that he interpreted them with unvarying accuracy. . . . The Conspiracy Theory of history and now of events. It was contemporary and fashionable but alas not always entirely convincing.

In any case he wasn't running.

10

The General had been sleeping badly for his conscience had been nagging tiresomely. Like all sensible men he kept firm control of it but there were occasions when it broke its disciplines. This was one of them and the reason distressful. He had eaten crow at Mahmud's hands and the bird had disagreed with his stomach. . . . A reprimand to Colonel Mahmud, a humiliation to his Commanding General! At the time he had felt a certain pride since his first aim had not been to pull his rank but to avoid the risk of a *coup* internally. This he had seen as his duty and done it, but he was also the country's most senior officer with the habits of thought of his rank and caste. It wasn't permanently acceptable that a junior should in effect dictate to him. He knew perfectly why the Crown had appointed him and that, at the time, had been quite in order. But now times had changed and it wasn't in order. All Generals had limits placed on their powers but that didn't make them some Colonel's creature. He'd been required to turn a blind eye and had done so but that didn't now make him a Young Lion's stooge. Why, he'd never even been out to his camp.

He decided it was high time he saw it, and to have any hope of proper judgment it couldn't be a formal inspection. He'd done many of these and all unreliable, the stones round the guardroom painted white, the stickmen and the parade of the good ones, the rest of them shoo-ed away on a route march, everything not up to scratch well hidden. A good

General learnt the tricks but not all of them, and the fact that there were tricks at all would be an irritant as well as misleading.

He took a driver and his Chief of Staff, driving along the new road to the camp, noticing even before he reached it that money had been no object whatever. There were no drunken posts with sagging wires but sunken conduits by the side of the road and inspection pits at regular intervals. A couple of roadblocks and both challenged promptly. It was a staff car flying the General's pennant but at both he had to identify properly.

Presently they saw the camp and the General permitted a long low whistle. He had known it was well-found and extensive but 'camp' in his mind had meant tents or huts. What he saw were modern concrete buildings, and the machines on their roofs spelt air-conditioning. In the background was a cluster of hangars and a helicopter was taking off, its rotors raising a fog of dust. At a break in the high wire fence was the guardhouse. The roadblocks had already telephoned, and when they saw the General's pennant the guard turned out and did it well. These soldiers didn't go stamp-bang-crash; they went clickety-click in a different tradition. The guard commander asked the General to wait. He had telephoned to the Colonel's office who would certainly wish to welcome him personally. He was already on his way in a jeep.

The jeep drew up sharply, raising the dust again, and Mahmud climbed out with his smart salute. He was in working order but clean and tidy. 'An unexpected honour,' he said.

There was something about his manner which galled. It wasn't presumptuous, far less impertinent, but he had the air of a man who'd been let off lightly and knew perfectly the real reason for leniency.

'Of course you will stay for lunch.'

'That's very kind.'

'Then if you'll follow me we can go to my office.'

It was nearly half a mile to headquarters and the General looked around him shrewdly. Men were moving at the double everywhere, not the high-kneed run of the penal parade but easily, at the pace they were used to. On the square there wasn't a soldier in sight. Already they were well past that; they had better things to do and were doing them. There was an ambience which the General recognized, indefinable but not mistakable. These men were relaxed, contented, purposeful. Colonel Mahmud might be a stubborn man but he was also a first-class commander of soldiers.

They went to his office and Mahmud served tea. Not coffee, the General noticed — tea. It was good ration tea, hot and strong and sustaining. The General looked round the room without seeming to. The furniture was brand new but simple, the walls bore maps but not of the Island. The only sign that the Island existed was a painting of the last head of its Order. The cross on his dishonoured habit had been painted out and left a blank. Mahmud said again:

'It's an honour.'

'You don't mind my looking around?'

'Of course not. What would you like to see.?'

'The aircraft. I can see that the men are in first-class fettle.'

They climbed into the jeep again, stopping beside the first of the hangars. The doors were open, the chopper beyond them, and under the arc lights a fitter had tools out. He wore a boiler suit and the standard black beret but the beret was without a badge. When he saw them he stood to attention rigidly. Mahmud said:

'That's my own machine, I fly her myself.'

. . . He's needling me. I do not like it.

'You appear to be able to do so skilfully.'

They'd been walking towards the machine to inspect it when the General stopped dead and stared at the fitter. 'Hassan?' he asked on a note of uncertainty.

'Sir!' the fitter said and waited.

The General promptly embraced him warmly; he did it in

Arab fashion, both sides. Then he withdrew two paces, smiling. 'Aren't you a little old for a soldier? I didn't know you'd re-enlisted.'

'I'm a civilian, sir, not a soldier again.' He spoke Arabic with a peculiar accent.

'Tell me the story.'

'It's happened before. When I drove for you I learnt something of engines so when my time was up I went to the airline. They took me and gave me a thorough training but when they nationalized it I wasn't happy. It was half-witted clerks trying to service aircraft. Mostly they were Our Guests, you see. So I left them and took on with him.' He nodded at Mahmud in open hostility.

The General was surprised but hid it. 'You're not happy here either?'

'The food is good and the pay even better but I don't take kindly to being insulted.'

The General couldn't pursue it there and then. 'When you come to the town you must come and see me. We'll talk of old times and of other places. You will take that as an order.'

'Sir!'

Mahmud looked at his watch and the General noticed it. 'Till then, old friend,' he said.

'Till then.'

Driving back to the mess the General told Mahmud: 'You probably guessed who that man was. I had him for many years as a driver and we had several and alarming adventures. Once we got lost in the desert — I thought we'd had it. We were down to half a pint between us.'

Mahmud said on a faint note of sarcasm: 'And he saved your life by giving you his bit?'

'No,' the General said, 'I gave him mine.' He hadn't liked Mahmud's sub-acid tone and added, as his rank allowed, a direct rebuff which was unmistakable. 'But you mustn't get melodramatic ideas. I didn't save his life as it happened because half an hour later some nomads came by, people of Hassan's own speech and tribe. Since then I have somewhat improved my map reading.'

The mess, like Mahmud's office, was simple, but the anteroom had comfortable chairs and all of it was air-conditioned. Mahmud introduced his officers. Several of them spoke very strange Arabic but all of them were lean and fit, all shared a common manner, an air of unquestioning dedication. In any other Brigade but this the General would have rubbed his hands.

He was climbing into his car after luncheon when he saw it and at once got out again. It was on the other side of the central road where Mahmud hadn't so far taken him. He pointed with his stick. 'What is that?' He was suddenly the General Officer, conscious of his rank and authority.

'It's a mock-up, sir.'

'I can see that, Colonel.'

'Would you care to inspect it?'

'Yes, very much.'

It was a mock-up of a city's square, the old buildings of painted canvas on wooden frames. There were houses and shops along three sides and the fourth was the front of a great cathedral. The painting was crude and bold but effective. The General knew at once where he was. He was looking at the Island's main concourse.

'What is this used for?'

'Practice in riot drill.'

It struck the General as careful planning. The Island's armed forces were less than formidable but its mobs could go berserk and wreck a whole quarter. When you'd brushed the former aside contemptuously you'd be vulnerable to the latter's fury. The Island's police wouldn't help you seriously so you must deal with the matter yourself.

And know how to.

'When's the next practice?'

'In half an hour.'

'If I may I will stay and watch it.'

'Yes sir. Would you like to go back to the mess?'

'No thank you.'

They sat in such shade as the canvas provided and the lorries began to arrive in a stream. From them descended what were presumably soldiers for they wore trousers and singlets and all were unarmed. Each of them carried a large basket of stones and most of them were grinning happily. Evidently this drill was popular. They took up station in the square and waited.

'The crowd, I presume,' the General said.

'As near as we can get to it, sir.'

A door opened in the cathedral's façade and a man came out in a shabby uniform. It was recognizably an Island policeman's. He began to make extravagant gestures, waving his arms and shouting gibberish. The crowd began to shout back rudely. So far the affair had been slapstick.

A bugler blew a G on his bugle.

Instantly there was a shower of rubble. It fell short of the policeman or went over his head. If it had not he would not have survived it.

'Very lifelike,' the General said. 'What now?'

Mahmud didn't answer but pointed. The crowd had begun to chant in unison, advancing across the square in menace. They were enjoying themselves and acting convincingly, the chants broken by occasional fierce yells. The General said again: 'A good show.'

But the soldiers were coming in now, packed tightly. They wore their helmets and carried riot shields and clubs. They advanced against the crowd which had halted. The two waves met, for an instant mingled. The clubs went up but they didn't come down.

There was another note on the bugle. Everyone froze.

'Does that conclude the entertainment?' The General had been impressed but was hiding it.

'That's as far as we can let it go, sir. These are quick-tempered men and we can't risk accidents.'

'No water cannon? Gas? Rubber bullets?'

'No sir, I've got no faith in those. They're no doubt effective against women and students but what we'll be facing is going to be neither. Short of shooting, which could end in a massacre, the only way to defeat your hard men is by physical contact with men even harder.'

It was an unorthodox doctrine and not in the book but the General didn't condemn it for that. He could see that it might one day be useful if his nightmare of a Guests' rebellion were ever to survive into daylight. But he was also very sure of one thing: this drill must never be tested abroad. Mahmud was further advanced than he'd thought. 'I see,' he said. 'I begin to see.'

They walked back to his car and he drove away.

In it he began to think furiously, for nothing of what he had seen had been comforting. He had expected to find fine troops and had found them, but he hadn't expected realistic riot drills. They must be very close to ready to go, and they might do so whether he liked it or not unless he risked the open challenge which he wasn't sure he could meet and win. He had many more men but they weren't like Mahmud's.

Which left him with a single alternative, and he wasn't a man to twist on the hook, looking for ways of escape which didn't exist. He didn't like Sayyid, he thought him too clever, but at least he had no soldiers behind him; he wasn't an insubordinate officer.

At his office he wrote him a simple short note, sending it sealed and by hand marked *Immediate*. The General begged to present his compliments and would be grateful if Sayyid would find time to call on him. Since the matter had more than a common importance he'd be even more grateful for prompt attendance.

Sayyid arrived a half hour later driving his modest Fiat himself. He'd been deep in a secret report on oil, how much there was likely to be and where, but a call from the General clearly took precedence. The General gave him a chair without ceremony.

'It was good of you to come.'

'My duty, Excellency.'

'No compliments, please. I have called you for business.'

The General had started in English and Sayyid followed. Arabic was a beautiful language, perfect for nuance and innuendo, but from the General's face he intended neither and English was much preciser for business.

'It would be seemly to call you "sir".'

'As you please.'

The General went on without changing his tone. It might have been an officers' conference. 'I should first make my own position explicit. I never sought political power but the manner of the Crown's sad death obliged me to assume it reluctantly. I am ready to give it up whenever I can. That means when it is safe to do so, when someone is able to pick up the reins.'

'I follow that,' Sayyid said at once.

'As a practical man I once saw three candidates, Suleiman, yourself and Mahmud. Now there are only two.' He held up his hand. 'On Suleiman's death I make no comment. Furthermore I ask no questions. The story in the newspapers was that some spark exploded his petrol tank. I accept that story.'

'Thank you, sir.'

'In any case his death was inevitable. A triumvirate was out of the question, but rule by diarchy would be equally dangerous.'

Sayyid had been listening carefully. By Arab standards this was indecently frank but he'd been educated at an Ivy League college and was prepared to put them down and count the pips.

'I agree that rule by two seldom works.'

'Which leaves me with two possible heirs and one of them I have come to mistrust.'

'May I ask your reasons?'

'I intended to tell you. The Crown had a plan to seize the Island and Mahmud intends to do the same. I always thought it a very great foolishness.'

That's the first big card, Sayyid thought; he would cover it.

'I always thought the same,' he said.

'Moreover Mahmud's force is powerful. I have good reasons with which I needn't worry you to fear that he might attempt a *coup*.'

Sayyid had considered this too but he hadn't considered the risk immediate. After all the General had armour: Mahmud had not. But the General didn't rattle easily nor talk of good reasons to cover the lack of them. Sayyid thought for some time and then asked quietly:

'You think his force could defeat your army?'

'I'd prefer not to take the risk that it might. There is more than one form of defeat, as you know.'

'You've been very frank, sir.'

'I saw no alternative. But I have a question to ask before I commit myself.'

'Ask it by all means.'

'Your own plan for the Island.'

'I never thought it worth a shot.'

'I never thought you did,' the General said.

Sayyid took time to make his decision. The General could hardly have heard of the oil, the secret had so far been too well kept, but equally he suspected some plan and a suspicious General would not play ball. He, Sayyid, was being offered support and if he fumbled now he could lose the prize. The General's backing was worth a secret shared.

'I don't want the Island. I do want its oil. Our own won't last for very much longer.'

'I didn't know that the Island had oil.'

'I would naturally have told you, sir, as soon as the position was clearer.'

'Why isn't it clear? It's clear to me. Either the Island has oil or it hasn't.'

'I'm afraid it isn't as simple as that.' Sayyid was being as smooth as silk. 'The oil isn't on the Island itself. It's half-way between us, under the sea.'

To Sayyid's relief the General took it; he not only took it, he understood. 'Where there might be disputes as to ownership?'

'Yes indeed.'

'And your idea is to acquire the lot?'

'If I can.'

'So in one sense you do have a plan for the Island. Not to invade it, we're agreed upon that, but to defeat any claim it may make on the oil.' The General pulled his white moustache. Privately he was immensely relieved. What he didn't want was a stupid war; he cared nothing for economic in-fighting; he said at last:

'I support that plan. I don't ask what it is since I know it's not military.'

He sent for coffee and both drank it quietly. When it was finished the General said amiably:

'I believe we have reached an understanding. I propose to resign as Head of State, nominating yourself as successor. How you consolidate that, how you get it legitimated, is something for yourself alone, but I intend to remain as chief of the army and if you run into trouble I'll back you fully. Call yourself President — whatever you fancy — but I suggest you don't choose the title "Crown".'

'I wasn't thinking of that.'

'I'm delighted to hear it.'

'You're really very kind.'

'Not at all.'

The words had had the faintest edge but if Sayyid noticed he let it pass. He lit a cigarette and smoked half of it. The General was already smoking.

'You realize, sir, that there's still a loose end?'

'Of course I do. By the name of Mahmud.'

'You will relieve him of his command?'

'I dare not. If I did so it might force his hand and tempt him into something regrettable. He might even start a civil war and in that there would be bound to be casualties. And if I'm right in something I think important we may need every man I've got in the future.'

'Our Guests, you mean?'

'What else could I mean? But this isn't the moment to talk

of that. The immediate problem is Colonel Mahmud.'

'Whom you dare not relieve of command?'

'That is so. However I could appoint a successor.'

Sayyid nodded at once; he had understood perfectly. 'And my side of the bargain is making that possible?'

'I don't lay it down as a term of the treaty. Nevertheless I ask you — could you?'

Sayyid thought it over carefully. 'Two bangs,' he said, 'would be somewhat corny.'

'Two bangs would be very corny indeed.'

'Difficult,' Sayyid said.

'I agree. Nevertheless the man flies helicopters, and choppers, like other aircraft, are vulnerable. When they run out of fuel they're obliged to land, in the desert perhaps, where survival is chancy, or over the sea where the odds are still poorer.'

'But surely they check their fuel gauges?'

'Yes.'

'So a competent pilot would know his limit?'

'He would if his fuel gauge were reading correctly.'

Sayyid said shortly: 'I couldn't fix that.'

'No, you could almost certainly not. But *I* might if I'm rather lucky.'

'May I inquire — '

'You may certainly not. Go and make yourself king. And I wish you good fortune.'

'The same to you, sir.'

'I'm going to need it.'

In the event it came his way in a flood for the fitter was frowning and muttering angrily as Mahmud, swinging his helmet, walked up to him. He'd been told to check the stabilizer and he'd done it only the day before. Moreover he didn't approve of flying alone. Nobody else was allowed to do so, and though Mahmud was the commanding officer the fitter thought him a very poor officer who would break his own rules for some private purpose. What that purpose was Hassan couldn't guess. Mahmud had been taking his aircraft up daily, flying it over the desert and bringing it back. Hassan, who was a first-class mechanic, could tell that each time he'd used the stabilizer. And the gun had been swung though it hadn't been fired. Against another rule it was always kept armed. An armourer saw to that but Hassan knew.

Hassan hated Mahmud bitterly for he'd humiliated him and done it publicly. Hassan was a civilian now but he'd been proud to serve in a fighting regiment and had put that regiment's badge on his beret. Mahmud had told him to take it out, he wasn't a soldier entitled to wear it. Hassan had controlled himself but he hadn't forgotten and never forgiven. He'd seen more service than this jumped-up boy, he'd seen combat and the other hadn't. He might be a civilian now but he had better title to call himself soldier than some Johnny Come Lately with two pips and a crown. He was a Berber who didn't accept an insult and the blood feud was deep in his heart and ethos. He'd never have the chance of revenge but if by some quirk if came he would take it.

When the chopper was airborne Hassan spat.

Mahmud was getting the feel of the stabilizer. He could fix it to make level runs, not long ones but long enough for his purpose, and he was making them lower each day as his confidence grew. With his hands free he could sight the gun. What had that damned Greek said of the timing? They went down to the Rabbit's Neck round about ten and by half past the hour they were in the water.

Today for the first time he'd practise firing, and he flew into the open desert till he saw what he wanted, two single bushes a few yards apart. They would serve very well for swimming bodies.

He brought the helicopter down and locked on. She was moving rather slowly ahead. He squatted behind the gun and worked the breech.

His first long burst was twenty yards short and the gun had been mounted to fire from the starboard door. He went back to his seat and turned for another run. This time he was equally over. He was firing in much longer bursts than his gunner would have thought professional but he saw that he still had enough for a final run.

This time he was dead on. He flew home.

Hassan knew the General well and when he had said 'Come and see me' he'd meant it. Hassan asked for and got a week-end pass and presented himself because he'd been ordered to. He had expected a chat of old times and there was one, but he heard something more which he hadn't expected, a proposition he accepted at once. He had the simple man's inflexible thinking and as he saw it he owed the General his life. The fact they'd been found in half an hour in no way diminished the gift of that water. Hassan had been in worse shape than the General and if they hadn't been found he'd have died before him. That water had meant they would die together.

So he listened, occasionally nodding happily. He asked no questions about the General's motives. These weren't his business; the accident would be. The General asked at the end:

'Will you need money?'

'I shan't need a penny.'

'I'm grateful.'

'So am I. For the chance.'

11

In Saliya the Greek was not highly considered but the snippets he sent were mostly reliable and the latest had been entirely accurate. Concerta and Russell were bathing daily and to do it he took her by car to the Rabbit's Neck. She had never been there before but Russell had, a deserted stretch of coast on the southern shore. The bay was beachless but perfect for swimming: you could wade from a shelf into deep warm sea. The Rabbit's Neck stretched out to the east of it. It wasn't much like the neck of a rabbit but the name had survived from Arab times and nobody had thought to change it. Beyond the Neck was another deserted bay and beyond that the new telecommunications centre. It was a jungle of masts and enormous antennae but astonishingly, almost eerily quiet. The road to it came from the further side, and once built it seemed to run itself. It was a rarity to see a man moving.

Russell left the car at the top of the bluff where there were now two new villas he didn't remember. The scramble down to the sea was quite steep, rather less than a cliff, rather more than a slope. Concerta was a biggish woman but she was sure-footed and as active as Russell. They had done this several times before and by now could almost have done it blindfolded. Once she slipped and laughed and he caught her arm. She tucked his under her own and went on.

They went down to the edge of the sea and sat down.

They'd discovered a ledge which was easy to swim from where the rock was pitted with ancient salt pans. They sat in their beach robes, legs in the water. Concerta said:

'You have been here before. You told me that but not the story.'

'War stories are mostly boring.'

'Not yours, I imagine.'

'Perhaps.' He considered. He'd been frightened and very near to death and the memory wasn't one he relished. Nevertheless he'd come back here — nostalgia. And Concerta was very much a woman; she'd pester him till she got what she wanted. 'Very well,' he said at last. 'Here it comes.' He collected his thoughts to tell it simply.

'I was on a destroyer going to Egypt and we were trying to sneak through to the south of the Island. The main convoys went much further north and, as you know, very little got through. The German air bases were uncomfortably close and the losses in convoy were very high. But for some reason I never knew we were sailing alone. I was supercargo and wasn't told much but I knew that the Captain had hoped to slip through. But he didn't — two German aircraft caught us. They carried torpedoes and one of them missed. But the second didn't — it caught us aft. There was a scaring explosion and clouds of steam. I didn't know a thing about ships but it was clear they'd hit the boiler-room squarely. We lost way and stopped; we were sitting ducks.'

'What happened then?'

'We started to heel. There were boats and rafts but the list was too great for them. I'd been told that the way to abandon ship was to go down the opposite side from the list so I slid on my bottom and there I was. Naturally I was wearing a life-jacket, but it wasn't summer. The sea was cold.'

'And after that?'

'Something very unpleasant. Those aircraft came down and gunned the survivors. To use an overworked phrase it was murder. I've never much cared for Germans since.'

'But they didn't get *you*?'

'As it happened, no, but I was one of the very few they didn't. When they went away I started to swim.'

'To the Island? How far?'

'Somewhere between a mile and two. I know it doesn't sound a lot but I had shoes on and that infernal life-jacket. Life-jackets keep you afloat all right but they're not designed for serious swimming. I kicked off the shoes but the jacket was difficult. It took a lot of my strength to get it off.'

'But you made it?'

'Just. I was as weak as a baby.'

'You landed here where we're sitting?'

'No I did not.' He waved an arm. 'I landed beyond the Neck, over there. And the rock there is higher, I couldn't get out. Perhaps I could have done it fresh, but I wasn't fresh, I was just about done. So I found a bit to hold on to and rest. I knew what I'd have to do and it frightened me. I'd have to start swimming again, round the Neck, hoping for lower rock the other side. And I doubted if I was going to make it.'

'But you did?'

'So it seems, but I don't remember much. I remember a little cave in the Neck where I got my feet down and rested a bit, and then I went on and remember nothing. Presumably I got out somehow for the next thing I knew I was lying in hospital. One of the gunners from up in the Battery had been taking a stroll and picked me up. Literally picked me up — he'd carried me. Across his shoulder, so he later told me. He was a very strong man but that bluff is quite steep. At the Battery they pumped me out and a doctor came out in a jeep from the hospital. I'd have had it if that man hadn't found me.'

Her comment caught Russell in disarray. 'I had the impression you didn't much care for us Islanders.'

He looked at her: she wasn't teasing. 'I can't say I much care for the Island — for one thing I don't like the way it's run. But I've a very soft spot for the people who live on it.'

'I'm an Islander too,' Concerta said.

He didn't answer her but looked away. He wasn't indifferent and he wasn't conventional but no spark had passed to fire more than acceptance.

When he looked back she was laughing quietly. Again she wasn't offended or angry; she seemed to be changing the subject but wasn't. 'What I really need is another Arab. They're very good in bed in their way. Unsophisticated but I don't mind that.'

'You can't spend the rest of your life in bed.'

'Nor do I intend to try. There's a terrible lot of rubbish talked about Arabs. They're supposed to treat their wives abominably and with one of their own they often do, but they're scared stiff of European women. That suited me fine — I like to be boss. All that *machismo* is just a front, you can twist them any way you fancy. And there's another thing which runs for you strongly: they're snobs and they're competitive snobs. The man with a European mistress is one up on the man with a fleet of Cadillacs. If she'll cook for him too he's a cock on a dunghill.'

'I can see there are compensations.'

'There are.'

'But must it be an Arab?'

'It seems so.' She looked at him again and now he looked back. 'No,' she said at last, 'but I'm sorry.' She laughed unexpectedly, took his hand. 'Come on, let's swim before it's too hot to.'

They went down to the sea where the rock shelved comfortably and soon were splashing each other like children.

Russell turned on his back and stared at the sky. A cormorant was flying low, away to his accustomed fishing grounds, and above him a flock of gulls mewed and wheeled. Above the birds was a speck in the sky, an aircraft. Russell rolled over and started to swim again.

When he looked again the aircraft was lower, a helicopter

with Saliyan markings. He was puzzled for it didn't make sense. He knew that these Saliyan aircraft were licensed to spy on NATO shipping but this was some way from the harbour they used for it. And the pilot was coming lower still, almost on to the sea itself. The chopper was moving forward slowly.

The first burst of fire missed Charles Russell by inches.

The warm southern sea felt suddenly polar as the sense of the unnatural gripped him. He'd been shot at off this coast once before and he knew that the human mind could play tricks. There were Holes in Space so why not in Time? He had fallen through the familiar world, floating frozen in an eerie noumenon. He'd come back from an anaesthetic once and the sensation had been the same paralysis. Till reality returned he was helpless.

Concerta swam up and touched him. 'Were you hit?'

He moved his head vaguely but didn't answer. She could see he was still treading water instinctively. What he could do beyond that she didn't know.

She looked up at the chopper in turn and shivered. It had risen to make its turn but was now descending. She dived pulling Russell with her. He didn't resist.

When she came up the chopper was past them but she could see that it was turning yet again.

. . . There's a cave in the Rabbit's Neck — he told me. Thirty or forty yards and it's coming back.

She got behind Charles Russell skilfully, hands under his armpits, her frog kick towing him. It was laboured and slow, Russell wasn't helping, and the chopper was almost on them again. Its pilot had read her intention correctly. Once under the rock he couldn't touch them and they were close enough now to make shooting difficult. If he continued an orthodox run he'd crash, for the Rabbit's Neck ended in naked cliff. The angle was now too acute for good shooting but the pilot was pouring it on while he could.

Concerta went on towing Russell. The pilot fired on

while he dared, then rose. His landing gear scraped the rock but he got away.

In the underhang there were four feet of water and Concerta propped Russell upright against the wall. She hoped that he hadn't swallowed much since she had neither the space to clear his lungs nor the strength to pull him back to the shelf. After crisis she had begun to react; she was trembling and the sunless sea felt suddenly unaccustomedly cold.

Presently Russell choked and coughed. He brought up some water but not very much. 'What happened?' he asked.

Concerta told him.

He was recovering, flexing his arms and legs. 'I don't think I'm wounded. I can't understand it.'

'I think you had some sort of blackout.'

'But I've been shot at before.' He was puzzled and angry.

'Let's talk about it later.'

'And you?'

'I'm having a pretty powerful reaction. I'm feeling as weak as a kitten.'

'We'll rest. I suppose that chopper has gone by now.'

She nodded. 'It might come back but I don't think it will. I heard it touch the rock above us.'

'You mean it crashed?'

'No, it didn't do that or not at once. The engine went on and I heard it fading. But it was more than a touch or I wouldn't have heard it.'

'Then he's probably damaged his landing gear, in which case he'll be making for home.' Russell looked at her again: she'd stopped shivering. 'Better to get back if we can. Can you manage it yourself?'

'Just about.'

They swam slowly to the shelf and got out, putting on their shoes and beach robes. They climbed the bluff without a word, sometimes Russell helping Concerta, often the other way round when he stumbled. At the top was their car and Concerta opened it. 'Get in,' she said. 'I think I'll drive.'

'That's a kindness upon a debt I'm unlikely to pay.'

In this assessment he was entirely wrong.

Mahmud had flown away frustrated: his intention had failed and he'd damaged his aircraft. The latter was in some ways the worse since he'd have to invent a story to cover it and he hadn't many gifts of invention. And that impertinent Hassan would hide a smile. Mahmud knew that the fitter didn't like him and recently his manner had changed. Once it had been correct though resentful — that absurd affair of the cap badge perhaps — but now it was almost the manner of triumph. Hassan was nursing some secret success.

Half-way across the sea the motor coughed. It picked up again but Mahmud frowned. He looked at his fuel gauge: it still showed a quarter.

A minute later the motor went finally. The helicopter began to lose height. The gauge was still showing a generous quarter.

Mahmud looked down at the sea. It was empty. Normally there'd be some sort of shipping but today there wasn't a vessel in sight. His fear increased as the chopper fell lower. He hadn't given away the fact that he meant to fly over the sea, not the desert, so he hadn't dared to wear a life-jacket. Like many Arabs he swam very poorly. The door had been taken off to fire the gun. Mahmud knew that she wouldn't float more than seconds.

The helicopter came down quite gently but almost at once she began to fill. As she settled he scrambled out through the door.

He had his boots on still and a heavy flying coat. He lasted perhaps three minutes but no more. He was a pious man as well as stubborn and as he drowned he commended his soul to his Maker.

When Sayyid heard of the death he nodded. The General had been as good as his word. He, Sayyid, was out in the clear, stripped for action. Ruthless, sensible, practical action, not some childish scheme to invade the Island. Who wanted that over-publicized Island? But Sayyid wanted its oil and would have it. He looked at the map on his table and smiled. If you accepted the Median Line where they'd drawn it the Island could claim a good half of the field.

Could claim it but it wouldn't succeed.

Sayyid had worked it out in detail, exactly as Father Gabriel had guessed. Intervention in other states was unfashionable, liable to raise frowns internationally. He cared little for the impotent statelings which interminably talked in New York and did nothing, and military action was surely unnecessary, a pipe-dream of the Crown and of Mahmud. Now both were dead he could act effectively.

For one thing a state could still do with approval, muted perhaps, but implicitly tolerated. If a country maltreated another's nationals, harassed them and burnt their houses, the second could use its best endeavours to protect its own people from molestation. Best endeavours, Sayyid thought sardonically — he had rather more than best endeavours. That oil would take time to come on stream but he could pull out the Island's cushion tomorrow. Its rulers had gone too far to withdraw, all its chickens were in one sack — Saliya's. . . . Back away from those unviable industries and none of them would last a fortnight. Stop the subsidy and they'd starve in a month. Tourism wouldn't keep them alone, and in any case there'd be no tourism, not with rioting throughout the Island. Bread riots. So it boiled down to a single card, an ace. Concede me all claims to that oil or I'll break you.

But was the Island maltreating Saliyans? Not yet. But that would be the easy part. Where they clustered in Xalah they were already unpopular: a respectable suburb was now a whore's parlour. They got drunk in public and pissed on walls. It shouldn't be very difficult to turn dislike into some overt action. Some violent provocation. . . .

Such as what? he'd once wondered. He had it now.

Obviously something to do with women. That was what Saliyans went for, women and drink but chiefly the women. Naturally they were Island women or Saliyans would not have bothered to go there. So Saliyans maltreat the Island women or in this case they appear to have done so. . . .

The Island mob had tasted blood, encouraged by its masters to do so. Once out of hand it might do anything, beat and burn and loot and murder. When Sayyid would be in the driver's seat firmly.

He could hear the exchanges loud and clear for he wouldn't need diplomatic double-talk, just a reference to the Median Line and another to Saliyan aid. The Fox would get the message at once. A continuing dispute on the former would mean that the latter ceased next day. So he needn't use diplomatic blah, but he was a Head of State now, at least in name, and there was a sort of old boy network between them. One didn't rub a man's nose in his faeces openly. He owed it to the Fox to save his face. So he'd leave him a couple of rigs to play with and if Allah were good they would both be dry.

He returned to the practicalities happily for he believed he had them cut and dried. Islanders were emotional people. If their women were beaten or better killed they'd give Sayyid a cast-iron excuse for action.

He couldn't trust that Greek to do it but it was easy to slip men in and out. It would be a mistake to overplay it to start with. Just one or two to light the fire, then others to feed the flames. Quite literally.

The highest strategy, he thought again, was not to win your wars, even quickly, but to have your ultimata accepted.

It was a policeman who found them face down on the pavement. The curved knives were in their backs, through the heart. He had seen a dead whore before more than once but not one who had died by an Arab dagger.

He turned the heads and looked at the faces. One was a hard old pro and he shrugged but the other was an amateur, the wife of a man who worked in the dockyard.

The policeman used his radio promptly. His Inspector wouldn't like this at all.

12

The Fox had liked it even less. He was sitting with what was in practice his Cabinet — Father Gabriel, Mortimer, the top man in the police. In Xalah the vigilantes were out and the Fox had received a deputation, an angry one from the dockyard workers. If the police could not protect their women — never mind what sort of women, just women — they'd feel free to take steps to do it themselves. The policeman said:

'It's fairly quiet so far — I've saturated the area. I've got every man I can spare on the streets.'

'I'm not happy.' It was Father Gabriel.

'Nobody's happy. It's extremely inflammable.'

The telephone rang and the Fox answered it promptly. 'For you,' he said to the policeman, who took it. He listened and put it down with a frown.

'An incident,' he announced regretfully, 'though happily not a serious incident. Some locals caught a Saliyan shopping. He was jostled and harassed a bit — nothing serious.'

'You don't call that serious?'

'No, not really.'

'I suppose it isn't but it's a straw in the wind.'

The phone rang again and again the Fox answered it. He was at his mildest and his most conciliatory, and when he rang off he said uneasily: 'That was the Saliyan ambassador. He's demanding a guarantee of his people's safety. That's routine no doubt, but one thing isn't. He's been remarkably quick on the draw, don't you think?'

'Remarkably,' the policeman said. The Fox ignored him and turned to Mortimer. 'And what do you deduce from that?'

'An element of organization.'

'Just so. And just what we have to fear.'

Father Gabriel broke in at once. This was running too close to his forecast to Russell. The others seemed to be thinking as he had but it was better to confirm that they were. 'So someone is planning trouble in Xalah?'

'Saliyans of course,' the Fox said angrily.

'To what end?'

'I don't know yet but I could make a long guess. And if I'm right it will not rest with this. Saliyan knives in a couple of tarts and a Saliyan mildly roughed up next morning. There's not too much mileage in that as it stands. But another major incident and Xalah could go up in smoke.' He turned to the policeman. 'You realize that?'

'I am doing my best.'

'Better make it a good one.' The Fox rose and dismissed the other two. 'But Father, I should like you to stay.'

When the others had gone the Fox asked softly: 'Do you think that policeman is up to his job?'

'I'm sure he won't do anything foolish such as catching a Saliyan murderer and embarrassing us by making us try him. In any case I'm sure he can't. Whoever used those knives is out by now. There was a ferry last night. I checked.'

'So did I. But what I meant was is he up to real trouble?'

'He can guess at its nature and make some plans but he hasn't had much practice, has he?'

The Fox flushed but he knew what the Jesuit meant. There'd been at least two disturbances, one of them serious, but the police had been ordered to walk very softly. One disturbance had suited the late Prime Minister and the other had suited the present Fox.

'Mortimer?' Father Gabriel asked.

'Not in his line — I wish it were. He runs what he calls the shop and he does it well. No doubt he could arrange a killing but we don't know where to look for a victim. And if we're guessing at anywhere near the truth a single elimination would hardly help. They'd go on pumping in men till they got what they wanted.'

'Which we're assuming is a major riot directed against the Saliyans in Xalah.'

'An excuse for some extreme demand which they know that we couldn't refuse. We've gone too far.'

'Are you thinking of any specific demand?'

'I'm thinking of the same one you are. I'm thinking about the oil and the Median Line.' The Chief Executive walked to the window and back again. He said more quietly than usual, almost humbly:

'I wish I knew some precedent. I wish I had something to guide me, fall back on. I confess to you, Father, I'm out of my depth.'

'May I make a suggestion, then?'

'Please do.'

'Colonel Russell is still on the Island.'

'Well?'

'He's a man of enormous experience. He knows more about international blackmail than any other man I can think of.'

'It would mean telling him the whole story.'

'Of course.'

The Fox thought it over for nearly a minute; at the end he said firmly: 'You have my authority.'

'He has asked me back to lunch today. He's a man you can talk to. I'll see what he says.'

It was Russell's turn to buy lunch and he'd stuck to the Polly. He thought that the Jesuit was quieter than usual but over coffee on the terrace he opened up.

'Do you read the local papers?'

'Not much.'

Father Gabriel produced one and Russell read. The headline said SALIYAN OUTRAGE and the editor was an outraged man. This newspaper mostly backed the government and was normally well on the right side of safe, but the deputation which had called on the Fox had not put its grievance in stronger terms than this paper was openly doing this morning. If the government couldn't protect its subjects the subjects must act for themselves and would.

Charles Russell said: 'That's dangerous stuff.'

'Then look at this.' It was another newspaper. Saliyan money backed and produced it but it was written in English on excellent paper. On most days it was straight propaganda, bland and insidious, written to please, but today it was harsh and even minatory. If Islanders thought they could go unpunished for assaulting and beating Saliyan citizens it would be necessary to teach them a lesson. A very sharp lesson indeed. Once for all.

'Were Saliyans really beaten up?'

'Nothing of the sort — just a scuffle. After those two dead whores were found we sent in police reinforcements promptly. A Saliyan was jostled a bit. That's all.'

'Then why write it up as a major incident?'

'To fit in with the rest of the orchestration. Their ambassador has been phoning the Fox.'

'I suppose he could hardly do less.'

'Maybe. But he did it with very unusual speed. May I ask you what you make of that?'

'Not much. It could be one of your Mediterranean storms, the sort that blows up from nowhere and dies in an hour.' Charles Russell reflected, then added reluctantly: 'On the other hand it might be sinister, a build-up to something much more serious. I'm not saying it is but I can't say it isn't.'

'Knifing two women is provocation. If there's any more provocation in Xalah no one can answer for what may happen.'

'From what I've seen of the place I entirely believe you.'

'I didn't know you'd been there.'

'Once. I was sorry for the people who live in it. It seems it was once a respectable suburb but now it's a well-organized brothel.'

'Just for the record it isn't brothels. Brothels are in the book as illegal. It's private enterprise but it *is* well organized. The women take the Saliyans' last penny. They're mostly rather nasty Saliyans, and apart from the whoring there's also the booze. Saliyans can't drink in their own mad country so they come here and they drink like animals. They fight and they foul the streets, they're a nuisance. Unhappily they also have money and you know how we love our tourists.'

'Quite. But not that kind, I rather think. Anyway, not the people of Xalah.'

'And when they put Arab knives in our women — '

'I take the point,' Charles Russell said. 'So what's happening in Xalah now?'

'Would you care to see?'

'Why not?'

'Then I'll show you.'

They took Russell's car and drove to Xalah. There was a police post on the road which stopped them, but the policeman recognized Father Gabriel. The car he wouldn't admit but he let them pass.

Russell shivered for he'd known this before, the smell of an Indian city before a riot. The bar where he'd drunk was boarded up and so were most of the shops and restaurants. The houses had their shutters closed and outside three or four there were vans. They were loading the household's furniture fast. There wasn't a Saliyan in sight but there were groups of Islanders idling on corners. There were police in every street and alley, patrolling in pairs and openly armed, but they didn't challenge the men on the corners. The numbers seemed about equal.

Bad.

Father Gabriel read Charles Russell's thought. 'Not all

these men come from Xalah. I wish they did. Many of them have come up from the dockyard. I think you know about that.'

'I know a little.'

'They backed the late Prime Minister blindly and on more than one occasion he gave them their head. They've tasted mob power and they know how to use it. One of the women killed was a matey's wife.'

They walked down the hill to the creek and sat on the wall. Here the tension was slightly less but not much. It was a bus route but today none were using it. The tide stirred the yachts in the little marina but all of them were entirely deserted. There were a few passers-by but they scurried uneasily.

Father Gabriel asked Russell: 'Well?'

'I'm not a policeman.'

'But I'd guess you've smelt this smell before.'

'If you're asking me what I think I'll tell you. If nothing more happens I would back you to hold it. But if another spark falls in the barrel you'd better pray.'

It wasn't a policeman who found them the second time but a prowling patrol of vigilantes. They heard a scream from an open window above them. Two men broke down the door and the third ran in. It was a house which let bed-sitters to prostitutes. In the first was a woman lying in bed and a man who was climbing out of the window. The vigilante tried to grab but he broke. He dropped from the window and ran through the yard.

The vigilante went into a second bedroom. Another woman was also dead. In the third she wasn't quite dead but dying. All three had been disgustingly mutilated.

The vigilante retched, then he joined the others. He made a couple of gestures — enough. Another man blew a whistle shrilly and in a moment there were over fifty. The police were simply brushed aside. They hadn't had orders to fire and didn't dare.

The telephone woke the head policeman at midnight and he listened to it as white as his bedsheets.

'How many did you say?'

'Seven dead, or seven so far.'

'Injured?'

'Maybe thirty or forty. And the place is in flames and spreading fast.'

The head policeman said: 'I'll come at once,' but he knew that it was out of his hands.

Charles Russell was also woken at midnight for the fire engines were thundering past, their sirens screaming in near-hysteria. He went to his bedroom window and looked west. In the sky was a nacreous pall of smoke bloodied by flashes of crimson flame.

He went back to his bed but not to sleep. He wondered about Father Gabriel. Was he praying as he'd been advised? It was possible. But more likely he had gone to the Fox.

Charles Russell was very glad he was neither.

Father Gabriel was indeed with the Fox, the lights blazing in the curtained room. On the table was a radio, tuned to the head policeman's wavelength, and the messages were still coming in. The faces of both men were grim. The Jesuit said:

'They're amok all right. A dozen Saliyans just clubbed to death. Wounded nearly fifty.'

'And rising.'

'You could send in the Forces.'

'Who wouldn't shoot. They haven't been trained to shoot their own people.'

The two men sat in frozen silence. Presently the Fox said miserably:

'We're going to get an enormous bill. It's obvious now that they planned it all carefully.'

'An ultimatum about our claims to that oil?'

'But first there'll be the humiliation. I'll be summoned to

attend on Sayyid. What's more I dare not decline to go. He'll play with me, cat and mouse, and then bang. Out with the terms which I'll have to accept.'

'What we need is a powerful ally.'

'We have none. The late Prime Minister himself fixed that finally.'

'I wonder,' Father Gabriel said.

'You mean you have some idea for action?' The Fox was so tired that he sounded uninterested.

'A rather thin chance but a good outsider.'

'What does it depend on?'

'Charles Russell.'

'How can he help? And if he can, will he?'

'I'm going to find out both at once.'

Russell had managed to sleep again and was annoyed to be woken a second time. Robert Mortimer stood by his bed in a dressing-gown.' That priest,' he said. 'He's demanding to see you.'

'At this time of night?' It was three in the morning.

'He says that it's very important indeed.'

'It had better be. Very well, send him up. If he chooses to call in uncivilized hours I'll be damned if I'm going to dress to see him.'

'I'll ask Lucia to send up a pot of tea.'

'I'd be more than grateful for that. One cup.'

Father Gabriel came in with a formal apology which Charles Russell considered a thought too formal. But he could see that the priest was stretched to his limit and he took no pleasure in others' misfortunes. He decided that he'd make it easy.

'We were talking about Xalah yesterday. Round about midnight I heard the fire engines. From the window I could see it was burning.'

'A dozen dead at least. Many injured.'

'So somebody threw a torch in the powder barrel?'

'The Saliyans provoked it themselves. I'm sure of it.'

'Why are you sure?'
'More Islander women murdered and mutiliated. What other motive than provocation?'
'Which has clearly succeeded.'
'All too well.'
'So you've come for my advice again?'
'No. For help.'
Charles Russell's surprise was not affected; he thought that the evident strain had taken its toll. This priest was on the rack and showing it, but also he loved his country and served it, and these were virtues Charles Russell respected. He couldn't just brush him aside with ridicule. Instead he said gently:
'How could I possibly help?'
'Through your friends. You have powerful friends in other countries.'
'I'm afraid you're a little out of date. I did once know powerful men. Not now.'
'You know the President of — '
'Don't say it! I do know a man I call Mr President but I met him on a private visit. He comes to London for clothes and discreet amusement and a very great nuisance he is when he does.'
'And in London you once saved his life.'
'How do you know that?'
'Your people hushed it up but I heard. I told you I ran the Fox's Intelligence.'
'You appear to do it rather well.'
'I also hear that he'd like to repay you.'
'Not rather well, extremely well.'
Lucia brought in a tray of tea. Russell had asked for one cup but there were two. He poured for Father Gabriel and waited. He was curious rather than seriously interested. The Mediterranean mind worked differently and the mind of the Church had a formidable ancestry. The Jesuit finished his tea and said:
'So I think you will follow.'

'I don't follow at all.'

'You want me to spell it out?'

'Yes please.'

Father Gabriel looked surprised but said: 'Your President is Saliya's neighbour. He dislikes them as much as we do and worse — they've been a thorn in his flesh for at least ten years. Also he runs a more powerful state. It may not have much oil but it does have men. He could put on very heavy pressure.'

'Counter-pressure in your interest?'

'Just so.'

'I take the point but why should he do so? In particular why should he do so now?'

'If *you* asked him he'd be discharging his debt.'

'A little, if I may say so, Jesuitical. In any case why should I ask him?'

'To repay your own debt. Your debt to this Island.'

'What debt to this Island?'

'An Islander saved your life. From drowning.'

'Your Intelligence is *very* good.'

Father Gabriel managed the first smile of the morning. 'No it wasn't Intelligence — not at all. Concerta naturally told her sister who equally naturally told her husband. Robert Mortimer works for the Fox, as you know, so his duty was to tell him. He did. In passing we're all extremely grateful that you let the matter lie as you did. We had plenty of worries without another embarrassment.'

'I knew that you had other problems. There seemed no point in stirring the dust up.'

'Many men would have.'

'But I'm not one of them.' Russell added without a muscle moving. 'I'm a man whom you've outmanoeuvred wickedly.'

'Don't put it like that.'

'I prefer the facts. And talking of facts let us have them straight. You're proposing a sort of three-cornered settlement. The President owes me a debt. Agreed. I owe the

Island a debt. Agreed. So I pay my debt to you obliquely by asking my friend to discharge his own. He's to take some action to help the Island.'

'That's about it.'

'Thank God I'm a protestant.'

Charles Russell was outraged but respectful. The squeeze had been neat and also final, a perfect exercise in moral blackmail. He got out of bed and began to dress. 'Have you a car here?'

'Yes, of course.'

'Then let's take it.'

'Where?'

'To that President's embassy. There'll be someone on duty who'll send by radio.'

13

Charles Russell had gone back to bed and as a result was a little late for breakfast. When he came down they were grouped round the radio and the messages were coming in steadily. The fires were still burning but the carnage had slackened. The pro-government newspaper was uneasily balanced between condemning another Saliyan outrage and an apprehension which it failed to hide that a crippling price would now have to be paid for a private revenge which had gone beyond decency. The Saliyan-backed paper was frothing noisily. In his office, though they didn't know it, the Fox was listening grimly to His Excellency the Saliyan ambassador. The Fox would present himself in Saliya to render an account immediately, and in the event of his declining to go His Excellency wouldn't answer for anything.

The doorbell rang and they could hear the maid go to it. Presently she came back looking scared, saying something to Lucia in Islander.

'She says we have two Arab visitors.'

'Have we indeed.' It was Robert Mortimer. He opened a drawer of his desk with his back to them and something went into his pocket smoothly. 'All right, I'll get it myself. Stay here.'

'Be careful,' Lucia said.

'I will.'

He came back trying to hide surprise and failing. With

him were two obvious Arabs. 'The smaller gentleman likes to be called Mr President but he doesn't like it mentioned of what. The big one is his personal bodyguard. Mr President claims acquaintance with Russell.'

'Surely I do.' He walked up and embraced him. Charles Russell didn't relish the gesture but he bore it with a cool urbanity. 'My friend,' the President said, 'I came at once.'

The strongarm sat down with his back to the wall and Russell made the introductions. The President bowed to Lucia and Robert but he took Concerta's hand and kissed it. Concerta had dropped her eyes but now raised them. 'Enchanted,' the President said.

'But equally.'

Lucia said: 'May I make you some coffee?'

The President stole a glance at his watch and Robert, an excellent host, saw him do it. 'Or perhaps you would prefer something stronger?'

'That's extremely kind.'

'Then how do you take it?'

'I take it straight. On the rocks, if I may.'

Robert Mortimer mixed the drink and returned with it.

'Aren't you drinking yourselves?'

'It's a little early.'

'Then I'm sorry I must drink alone but I've suffered a rather trying journey.' The President took a long pull at the whisky. Over his glass he was watching Concerta. He was his usual ebullient extrovert self, as different from the traditional Arab as a man could be without hamming the difference.

If indeed, Russell thought, he was an Arab. There were plenty who would deny it strenuously. 'How did you get here?' he asked.

'By air.' He stopped Russell as he started to speak. 'Do not fear, it's a very modest aircraft — no coats of arms, no pompous inscriptions. Unlike another's whose name we won't mention.' He was as gay as a bird and still watching Concerta; he said to her:

'I'm a wicked man. I loathe visits of state and avoid them persistently. I travel incog and that isn't done. I go to London to buy my clothes and enjoy myself, where I'm a headache to every form of Security. Last time I went I was something more. But I won't be bothering anyone here. I'll be away in a couple of hours at most when I've had a little chat with Russell.'

'But surely at Immigration — '

'Oh no. I've a passport in my own modest name and the photograph is not in focus. I also wore a pair of dark glasses and a perfect fool I felt with them on. We walked straight through and intend to walk out again. The aircraft is refuelling now. I managed a few hours' sleep and I don't need more.'

His usual form, Russell thought. He said nothing.

'You have business with Colonel Russell?' Lucia asked.

'I have. But it won't take a moment.'

'You would like us to leave?'

The President looked at Charles Russell who shrugged. 'Between them they know as much as I do.'

'Good. Then we can talk freely.' He turned back to Russell. 'I got your message.' His manner had notably sharpened and hardened. He wasn't the volatile playboy now but the President of a state with some teeth. 'There's some trouble with those damned Saliyans?'

'They have us by the short hairs.'

'I imagine. Your late Prime Minister asked for it. Now it's come.'

'That doesn't make it easier.'

'Quite. But I like them no more than you do. The Crown made three attempts to kill me but it's more important that they discriminate against my nationals who hold their country together. So I repeat that I like them no better than you do. Shoot.'

Charles Russell explained with a crisp lucidity and at the end the President said: 'And so. And so you would like me to help you?'

'Would you?'

'Certainly, but I don't yet see how.' He began to talk at large, eliminating. 'No doubt I could take them over by force. My army isn't a very good one but compared to theirs it's almost invincible. They have just two good regiments with up-to-date training but their Colonel crashed at sea and drowned. Something fishy about that, by the way, but to return to the point I don't dare invade them. It would tear the Arab world apart and I've enough on my plate elsewhere already. On top of that I have friends further east whose subsidies keep my country breathing. They'd treat me like a Victorian parent and cut me off with the proverbial shilling.' The President shook his head. 'That's not on.'

But he hadn't yet concluded his homily. He looked at his empty glass and Mortimer rose. This time the other two men drank too.

'On the other hand there's old-fashioned sabre-rattling—move troops to the frontier, make menacing noises. But that would be bluff and would be seen to be bluff. Moreover it's very expensive too and open to the same objection that my paymasters would kick again. Nevertheless I do have a weapon.'

He looked round inquiringly: nobody spoke. The President drank some more whisky thoughtfully. He was enjoying himself. They were silent as Trappists.

'My weapon is sharper than Arab armies, a fifth column in Saliya itself. I have twenty thousand nationals there, mostly working in the jobs which matter. And they've a permanent and justified grievance since they're not paid the going rate for the job. They demonstrate from time to time and recently some fool got shot. But there's been nothing really serious yet. If there were they could bring the state to a standstill.'

Russell asked softly: 'You'd smuggle in arms?'

'Not at first I wouldn't — no, certainly not. But I'd send in some men who knew their business, not cheerleaders to be picked off at leisure but men who know how to organize discontent. Men who know how to make crowds formidable.'

'You intend to give the Saliyans a fright?'

'But I'll give them a warning first. I've a man there.'

'A warning of what?'

'My extreme displeasure. It will be put in diplomatic terms since my man is a professional diplomat but I'll instruct him to make the message clear. The Median Line is the line through the middle. Go further than that and you've made an enemy, an enemy whose resident nationals can grind you to a halt if they're told to.'

'It's tough,' Russell said.

'Aren't you?'

'I'm a realist.'

'To whom I owe a debt which I'm anxious to pay.' The President stared at Charles Russell, unsmiling. '*You* are asking this? I don't inquire why.'

Put to the question Charles Russell hesitated. He was about to break a principle, never to get involved in another state's politics. He had broken it before more than once but only when he'd been free to withdraw. As he wasn't he decided, now. He knew that Concerta was watching him closely and previously she'd been watching the President. If he reneged on his debt she'd think him contemptible. Moreover she'd have good reason to do so. He said finally:

'I am asking.'

'Right.'

The President stood up immediately, his earlier casual manner returning. 'Then I'll leave at once and do what I can. There's a word for this and it's intervention but I prefer to call it Russian diplomacy.'

Robert Mortimer said: 'We'll see you off.'

'I beg you to do nothing so foolish. I came in as a tourist — a fortnight stamped on my private passport.' He produced it in almost boyish triumph. 'And tourists aren't seen off by attendant courts.' He added in his cavalier manner but looking at Concerta levelly: 'Just one friend perhaps to wish them well.'

Concerta got up at once. 'Very gladly.'

'Then I'll call a taxi,' Mortimer said.

'No need to. I kept the other waiting.'

When the President and Concerta had gone Mrs Mortimer said to her husband: 'Well!'

He was irritated. 'Well what?'

'You're an extremely unobservant man.'

They were sitting having drinks before dinner when the maid came in and bobbed politely; she said with an air of resignation:

'Another Arab gentleman, madam.'

'What does he want?'

'To speak to Miss Concerta, please.'

Robert Mortimer asked: 'Would you like me to come with you?'

'No thank you. I can handle Arabs.'

On the doorstep was the well-dressed young man who had previously twice called on Russell. He was carrying two dozen red roses. 'For you,' he said. He handed them over. 'Ordered from the aircraft in flight. I'm sorry there was a delay in finding them. This isn't a part of the world where they grow well.'

'It isn't indeed. Please send my thanks.'

She didn't return to the others but went upstairs. She found a vase and arranged the roses, staring at them with a secret smile. At the airport he'd made her a proposition, sitting there in those ridiculous glasses, the strongarm on the seat beside him. The proposition had been extremely generous and she had liked the way he had made it too. No protestations — a straightforward bargain. But she hadn't been perfectly sure he had meant it.

Now she was sure and of something else. Her own answer would equally surely be Yes.

The President's man in Saliya had done his job. Sayyid had moved to the ancient palace since as State Protector (he had chosen that title) he culd hardly continue to live in two rooms. The interview should have gone off smoothly for the ambassador was an accomplished career man, but Sayyid had been less experienced and his mask of bland courtesy cracked the first.

The ambassador had begun on a note of regret. His country had a longstanding friendship with brother Arabs in the state of Saliya and it was therefore to be regretted deeply that at the moment there was a divergence of policy.

Sayyid had bluntly asked what policy.

That oil in the channel, the Median Line. The Island was now an Arab colony in everything but the formal name but it was also a drain on Arab resources. Would it not be a better plan to allow it some modest prosperity of its own?

Sayyid had said that in theory it might be but that he needed that oil for himself and immediately. His country hadn't as much as some people thought.

But surely with proper negotiation . . . ?

The matter was in no way negotiable.

Was that a final decision?

It was.

The atmosphere had cooled at once for neither man much liked the other. The ambassador thought Sayyid was too much westernized, a man who had lost his native loyalties in the interests of something called civilization. Sayyid, an upper-crust Bedu Arab, thought His Excellency was an evident cad. He must be to serve that detestable President. Moreover his complexion and features were suspect of other blood than Arab. In the State Protector's private vocabulary there was a blistering word for such as His Excellency.

'You really do not feel that some compromise . . . ?'

'I regret there is no room for compromise.'

His Excellency's manner promptly froze. Then in that case the matter was past diplomacy.

The State Protector made a serious mistake. Instead of expressing regret again he permitted himself a wordless shrug.

The ambassador rose instantly, protocol and training forgotten. He was simply an insulted man. 'You are not in a position,' he said, 'to act against my President's wishes.'

The situation was still reparable by some formula about consulting colleagues but Sayyid did not love his visitor. In any case he disliked being browbeaten. He made his second mistake, the mistake of sarcasm.

'You were thinking of taking us over?'

'Certainly not.'

'Then if I may ask it — '

'You'll soon find out.'

His Excellency withdrew in anger and Sayyid, from the balcony, watched him go.

He stayed for a moment, now watching the square. It stretched below him, untidy and crumbling. A gardener was pottering idly, engaged in the hopeless task of trying to raise flowers. A row of decaying carriages stood waiting for custom which seldom came, the horses half asleep between the shafts. The houses which formed three sides of the square had their plaster in ribbons and filthy doorsteps. Slatterns' washing hung on lines in the balconies. The city had fine, even opulent, suburbs, where the newly rich lived on the money from oil, but this was where Our Guests lived. Damn them. They'd even had to gall to demonstrate. Sayyid hadn't been there but the General had told him. A single shot and they'd run like rabbits. Sayyid didn't fear the Guests. They were leaderless and wholly unorganized.

A fortnight later he was changing his mind, standing in the still splendid salon, hidden behind its curtains but facing the square. The General had been summoned by telephone and he'd come in, as he'd done before, the back way. He didn't condescend to conceal himself but walked straight to a window and stood there unmoving.

He didn't like what he saw for this time it was different. The square was full of people again but now there wasn't a woman among them. There were the same banners with the same demands but no chanting, no obvious leader to shoot at. There was an utter silence which scared the General since a silent crowd was one under discipline. And there were other signs of organization. The men weren't packed together tightly but stood in separate groups like military squares. He couldn't see any signs of firearms but most men had staves of a uniform pattern. For a moment a group broke ranks and then formed again. It had done so to let out a man who had fainted. The break had been short but enough to disclose it, the pile of stones and bricks at the centre. This crowd meant trouble, serious trouble, and was organized to make it effectively.

The General looked at the crowd again. It was younger than before and stood steadily. A single shooting wouldn't clear them.

Sayyid came up behind him, said: 'Well?'

'I think we are in for a major disturbance.' The tone was deliberate, almost judicial. Armed men would have little advantage against those squares. Unless, of course, they were ready to shoot, and the General had a soldier's distaste for indiscriminate shooting at unarmed men. One man had been different, an execution, regrettable but also necessary. A massacre he would not condone.

Sayyid had begun to tremble. The General could see it was not with fear but with a furious frustrated rage. He'd been State Protector for only weeks and already the Guests were challenging openly. He'd lost face and that was something precious. He said in a voice which wasn't steady:

'What are you going to do?'

'That depends.'

'Depends on what?'

'On what you decide to do yourself. If you ask me those men have a very real grievance.'

'I did not ask you.'

Sayyid had lost control of his anger. He despised the Guests to a man; he loathed them. He said in his still unsteady voice:

'I order you to clear the square. Fire till it becomes so. At once.'

The General said: 'I hear the words.'

The shock of the insult sobered Sayyid. 'You are refusing an order?'

'The order is political suicide. If I order men to shoot you're in trouble. Very grave trouble — you know from where. Those men are not Saliyan citizens. There's a powerful state behind every one of them and I suggest that they have the right to be heard.'

'You mean I should speak to them?' Sayyid asked it in bleak astonishment.

'Yes I do.'

'I'd rather die.'

'You will do that some day.'

There'd been something in the frayed old cliché, an undertone which froze Sayyid rigid. He was being called a coward and he was not.

'You think I should go out and talk to them?'

'I consider you have no alternative.'

'Will you come if I do?'

'Of course I will.' The General was curt. He didn't fancy a public stoning but he couldn't refuse a second order, not one which would reflect on him personally. Sayyid opened the door and they both went out.

. . . I have been here before but that was different. A few sporadic stones and a lot of noise. A single man killed and everything over.

Not today.

Sayyid threw up his arms and began to speak. The gesture was unnecessary since already there was total silence. He was an orator and he began to orate. A few simple words might perhaps have appeased them but he was talking in generalizations, fluffing it. For perhaps half a minute nothing happened, then unmistakably came a concerted raspberry.

Sayyid went scarlet and silent together. The General wasn't watching him; he was watching the two front squares intently. They had opened, revealing their piles of rubble. They hadn't torn it up; they had brought it.

They threw in volleys, controlled and accurate, obedient to some inaudible order. The first was a little too high but not much. The plate-glass windows behind them disintegrated. Sayyid had already fallen.

The General went down too, though reluctantly. For the moment the balustrade was protecting them but the stoners could always move nearer and lob. He could see that Sayyid was lying face downwards and he began to crawl towards him quickly. A brick caught him in the small of the back. The General grunted but went on crawling.

He turned Sayyid face upwards: it was more than enough. The top of his head was a livid pulp.

The General pulled the body inside, then rose himself and went to the telephone. The man he'd appointed in Mahmud's place had been carefully chosen as safe and reliable. He didn't have any ambitions of conquest but he wouldn't have let good troops deteriorate. And those troops had a riot drill— the General had seen it. They'd been trained what to do without causing a massacre.

The irony for a moment amused him but the stimulus didn't sustain his smile. Sayyid's death had put him back in the saddle and the ride was going to be rather less than comfortable.

14

Lucia was in Concerta's room, noting the fresh bowl of roses. The two sisters had the perfect relationship, affectionate and understanding, but with an occasional flash of sub-acidity to keep the mixture from cloying the palate. Lucia was saying:

'You must be out of your mind.'

'That's nonsense. He has made me a very generous offer. I'd be out of my mind to turn it down.'

'How generous?' It was an Islander asking it.

'A villa and an adequate income.'

'And when he gets tired — '

'As he surely will. I'm not the fool you think me, sister. There's a nice bit in a Swiss bank already. That was a bit of a gamble on his part but he realizes that I'm gambling too.'

'He must be very rich.'

'I imagine so. All politicians make money somehow.'

'You mean he's bent?'

'Of course he's bent. Not in the sense that matters, though.'

'No, I didn't mean that.'

'Then next question please.'

It came as a sisterly shaft, half playful. 'No doubt you know all about Arabs.'

'Most of it. I've had wider experience than you, Lucia.'

'Including cutting your gentleman's head off.' This time the arrow was aimed directly.

It bounced off without damage. 'Oh that! He knows. He'd heard some rumour so I told him the story. We had an hour at the airport to chat and I used it. He looked a bit surprised, then he waved it aside. He said that I'd done him a personal service, to say nothing of the world at large. The Crown, you remember, had had three goes at him.'

'You seem to have used that hour pretty profitably.'

'I think it's a very fair agreement. There's nothing for me here on this Island. His capital is cosmopolitan and I'll have a respected if not quite respectable position.'

There was a pause before Lucia said softly: 'I'd wondered — '

'About Russell? So had I. I gave him some very unmaidenly openings.'

'I bet you did.'

'Let's leave it, then. I'm afraid I'm a rolling stone, my dear, so I might as well roll in a little moss.'

'You seem to have gathered that all right.'

'I'm glad you approve.'

'But I didn't say that. I'm a respectable, catholic married woman. What you're doing is living in sin with an infidel.'

'Do I sniff the faintest smell of envy?'

'No, you do not. Of course you don't.' But it wasn't pronounced with a total conviction. A pause before:

'Then when are you going?'

'Tomorrow morning. He's sending his own aircraft to fetch me.'

'Be happy then.'

'I can hope for contentment.'

The General was taking a bath and frowning. He was stuck with it again and loathed it. Some day if God were willing and kind a man would appear to take up the burden but for the moment he must bear it again. Maybe it was less than once for he'd been to see the President quietly and they'd struck the bargain of pragmatic men. What the General did with that wretched Island was in no way his neighbouring

President's business provided he didn't attempt to seize it. . . . That oil was going to be dealt with amicably? The President thought that a proper solution, so sensible he could himself act sensibly. Those Guests. for instance, need offer no problem. . . . The General already sympathized? Excellent. Then their wages could be raised to parity and in return there'd be no trouble internally, far less an excuse for intervention.

And of course, he had added, a trifle slyly, he himself must be free to drive in unarmoured cars.

They hadn't needed to put it in writing, but the General had smiled a little wanly.

His roses were further away than ever.

Charles Russell was packing his unfashionable suitcase and Mortimer was at the bedhead, talking. Russell preferred to pack alone but Mortimer was his host and privileged. 'We shall miss you,' he said.

'I'll miss you too.' It was a social lie and as such told smoothly, but in fact he was very pleased to be going. A sense of sharp humiliation was nagging at his peace of mind. He'd been drawn into affairs before which he hadn't had any wish to enter but had returned from them with a smile or a shrug. He'd been persuaded or maybe events had compelled him but he hadn't before been morally blackmailed. He wanted to leave this Island behind him.

But Mortimer was talking on. 'The Fox wanted to thank you before you went but I told him you'd much prefer to go quietly.'

'You told him correctly. I'm much obliged.'

'Oddly enough he wasn't offended. A month or two ago he'd have thrown a rage but in the last few days he's grown up considerably. But I was to tell you how things stood.'

'Very well.' It sounded on the edge of boredom.

'That General has had to take over again and he was always dead against an invasion. The Saliyans who used this place as a brothel have gone and I doubt that they'll ever come back. Xalah can be rebuilt in time.'

'What will you use for money?'

'Oil. The General is a reluctant ruler — all he wants is to govern while govern he must. An international row about oil would only add to what he regards as a duty, so the Median Line goes to arbitration. From the latest reports the Fox has seen we should get enough oil to float us off.'

'To float you away from Saliyan influence?'

'Personally I rather doubt that. The late Prime Minister gave too much away. But enough to give us a voice of our own. And I'd guess the Saliyans had learnt their lesson. Another major riot and they'd fall apart. Next time the Guests might have arms.' He left it. 'No more blackmail by greedy men like Sayyid.'

Charles Russell said dryly: 'You're both pretty good at it.'

Robert Mortimer let this pass in silence; he looked at his watch. 'We'd better be going.'

'I'd be grateful for a lift to the airport but you're to drop me there and not hang about.' He added, looking the other way: 'Like your benefactor, my friend the President, I loathe the people seeing me off at airports.'

'Except an attractive woman.'

'Which you are not.'

There was half an hour to wait at the airport and Russell went upstairs to the bar. The place was still in total chaos, the bar was crowded, the service surly. Father Gabriel saw him and rose from a table.

He was the last man Russell wished to speak to and for a moment he considered discourtesy. But in the end he nodded coolly.

'Good morning.'

'May I offer a drink?'

'Thank you, but it's a little early.' Russell wanted a gin and tonic badly but he did not wish to drink with Gabriel.

'I came here to thank you.'

'Spare me embarrassment.'

'Then to give you some information.'

'I have it.'

'Robert Mortimer ran over it, then? We're not entirely out of our shackles but at least the clanking will not be too audible.'

'With your own remarkable skills I'm sure not.'

Surprisingly Father Gabriel laughed. 'Whoever is going to use skills it won't be me. As Mortimer told you we can stand for a while, so I'm no longer the Fox's man. I've resigned. I'm going to be a priest again.'

'You're going back to teaching?'

'No. I couldn't honestly teach again, or not the sort of thing I'm supposed to. I'm going back as a simple *parocco*, an ordinary no-nonsense parish priest. It's going to be a great relief; it may even save my compromised soul. Adultery, wife-bashing, skipping your Masses — the honest sins of common men. You've no idea how soothing they'll be after the envy, hatred and malice of politics.'

'That I can imagine.'

'Thank you. So starting on parish duties with you, you told me once you were not a catholic.' For once the smile was less than professional; it might almost have been apologetic. 'Then according to the book you're lost but between ourselves I no longer believe it. I think you're a good man and I thank you. I don't think you'll suffer for long. Good-bye.'

He didn't offer his hand for he wasn't insensitive. He rose and quietly walked away.

On the aircraft Russell sighed contentedly, the sense that he'd been exploited fading as the Island faded from sight behind him. Under the crust of his cool urbanity was a humour which was often impish, sometimes as now as black as night. He began to laugh softly, his neighbours staring. . . . A man was as young as he felt? That was nonsense. A man was as young as events permitted. Like all vigorous men he had thought of retirement as something which must be actively filled if old age were not to win indecently, but whichever angel kept his diary had been generous when it came to commitments. He didn't seek them: they arrived on his doorstep. This one had meant he'd been morally blackmailed but the weapon had been used with skill. It was absurd to resent it, plainly pompous, and pomposity was a vice he detested.

Another spasm of laughter shook him and he stood up from his seat to catch his breath. A hostess was on him at once to beat his back. Her manner was exactly right. She wasn't motherly, he was still a male, but she was something more than merely considerate.

'A choke?' she asked when he had his breath back.

'You could call it that. I beg your pardon.'

'Shall I get you a glass of water?'

'No thank you. But I'd like a glass of brandy, please.'

'The trolley — ' she began and stopped. Charles Russell had sat down and was smiling. 'Brandy it is,' she said. 'I'll get it.'

'I have something rather special to celebrate. I've been twisted round a better man's finger but I'm not going to let it disturb my sleep.'